The Vines of Ferrara

Also by Carolyn Coker

THE OTHER DAVID

The Vines of Ferrara

A Novel of Suspense

Carolyn Coker

DODD, MEAD & COMPANY

New York

7708

Copyright © 1986 by Carolyn Coker

Published by Dodd, Mead & Company, Inc.
79 Madison Avenue, New York, NY 10016
Distributed in Canada by
McClelland and Stewart Limited, Toronto
Manufactured in the United States of America

First Edition

1   2   3   4   5   6   7   8   9   10

Library of Congress Cataloging-in-Publication Data

Coker, Carolyn.
The vines of Ferrara.

I. Title.
PS3553.O4367V5   1986   813'.54   85-30764
ISBN 0-396-08812-0

The Este castle in Ferrara
is open for viewing on a schedule
that is noted in most tour books.
The Gonzaga castle existed
only long enough to accommodate
the characters in this book,
then disappeared.

One

The laws of nature did not seem to be strictly obeyed on the land that belonged to Geoffredo Gonzaga in Ferrara. Not, at least, the law of gravity as it applied to the wild grapevines.

The vines were the one exception. The feet of the vineyard workers always returned to the land, the wheels of the transport trucks clung to the gravel road from the fields to the winery, leaves fell to the earth in the fall, roots dug into it in the spring, and water did exactly as was expected of it in seeking the center of the earth.

Water, indeed, performed one of gravity's showier feats. It bubbled up from a subterranean spring at the top of the hillside garden, fell into a narrow, tile-lined trough, rushed through ancient ceramic pipes to an ornate fifteenth-century fountain at the bottom of the hill, gushed from the mouths of bronze fish, splashed at the feet of a statue of Neptune, drained into an irrigation system, seeped into the carefully cultivated fields of the vineyards, and finally, ran into the Po River on its way to the Adriatic Sea.

But the wild vines, the ones that crept up the crumbling

rear wall of the Castello di Gonzaga, defied both man and nature.

For generations they had been chopped back and buried. But still, they encroached and pushed, reincarnated from season to season. They climbed the dead stones and slithered through crevices with spiraling tendrils that reached skyward as though attached to taut strings the eye could not see.

When Geoffredo Gonzaga inherited the property, like his father and his grandfather before him, he gave orders to keep the vines cut back. But there were always little green shoots that slipped by, that found a slit between a door and the tile floor, or a tiny open space between an ill-fitting window and its casement.

The young woman in the black, starched maid's uniform knew about the stubborn vines. In summer, as a child, she had played in the fields while her mother corked and sealed bottles in the winery. And sometimes the children of the *cellerari*, the workers in the winery, were given hoes and told to clear the steep slope next to the castle where the tractors that turned the earth of the vineyards could not go.

But tonight the girl was working *inside* the castle of Count Gonzaga, an assignment from the Temporary Domestic Service Company of Ferrara. If her mother were still alive she would be proud of her daughter. *Molto orgoglioso*, very proud, to see her in sheer stockings and a white organdy apron.

The girl smiled to herself. She wondered how the man who had made love to her the night before in the vacant room next to the wine cellar would feel when he saw her again in the castle.

Not that she really cared about the man; she barely knew him. And certainly not that she hoped to marry him.

She knew that would never happen. But it had been amusing to say, "I'm the one who should be the owner of the castle. Then I would invite you to be my guest."

She had been surprised, even a little frightened by his intensity when he asked her to explain what she meant.

She had told him, without adding that she did not plan to live the life of her mother. She would not work in the vineyards or the winery and secretly covet the Castello di Gonzaga as her mother's family had for generations. Nor was being a maid the height of her career aspirations. But work from the temporary service paid her tuition while she attended the Scuola Superiore de Cosmetologia.

Thinking of her future gave her pleasure. It would be a world of sweet-scented shampoos, sharp, shiny scissors, well-shaped and sparkling fingernails. Working in a profession that made women more beautiful was any number of rungs above grubbing in the vineyard.

She glanced at her wristwatch in the moment she took to admire the California Sunset Glacé she had applied to her own nails. She had been told to be at the castle that morning at ten, but she was early. There was still no one else in the kitchen.

Idle hands, well-manicured though they were, seemed sinful and contrary to her early training. And so she consulted the large blackboard near the pantry door. The chef had listed the duties to be performed by the kitchen staff in preparation for a reception that evening to honor Count Gonzaga's brother Carlo from America.

Silver trays were to be polished, table linen ironed, shrimp boiled and deveined, Sangiovese di Romagna fetched from the cellar. Though her name was written next to the last task, someone had already done it for her. Six dusty bottles of the private vintage stood on the marble countertop.

She found a clean cloth in the cabinet under the sink, dampened it, and carefully wiped the dust from each bottle. As she finished the last one, she examined the lead seal that covered the cork and encircled the top of the bottle's neck. There were two tiny scratches; her mother's initials. A lump of sadness and the taste of disgust rose in the girl's throat as she realized that her mother had taken pride in her work, had wanted to leave her mark. Was this her epitaph in memory of the years spent blistering under the sun in the Gonzaga vineyards and shivering in the damp clamminess of the winery? Had she, the girl wondered, ever even tasted the wine she helped produce? Had she been invited to share a glass of the Gonzaga winery's finest vintage before it was bottled and sealed and stored away for the private use of the family?

Perhaps her mother had never tasted the famous Gonzaga Sangiovese, but the girl decided she would. Later she would bring up another bottle from the cellar to replace this one, she thought, as she deftly removed the seal with the scratched-on initials.

Dozens of crystal wineglasses were stored on a high shelf in the pantry, but this private ceremony deserved something finer. Inside a lighted cabinet in the hall that led to the dining room was a collection of antique Venetian glass.

The girl stealthily made sure she was not observed, then took a goblet from the top shelf and hurried back to the kitchen.

The exquisite long-stemmed glass was opaque and red in color with a single design. In a circle on the side of the bowl was a red bull standing in a golden field.

She held the glass by the foot as she had seen members of the Gonzaga family do, and poured in enough of the pale red wine to taste.

First she held the goblet beneath her nose, deeply inhaling the sweet aroma. Then she tilted her head back and drained the mouthful she had poured, first swishing it around her teeth and under her tongue, then letting it slowly slide down the back of her throat.

The fleeting smile of accomplishment lasted only until the wine reached her stomach. Then she felt, in quick succession, spastic contractions that made her throw one arm across her abdomen as though to press out the pain. Her heart pounded. The thin black fabric of the uniform that covered her young breasts lifted and fell as the beating, throbbing of her heart became faster. Air! Dear God, she had to have air! Her throat contracted and closed entirely as she made frantic, open-mouthed panting sounds. She stumbled, head down, toward the kitchen door.

The steps were treacherous, but she knew them. As a child, she had climbed them many times with baskets of fresh vegetables to be left on the stoop. She had counted the steps: seven. The fifth was narrower than the others. Even in her agony she was careful where she placed her feet.

Perhaps she could have stayed erect a few seconds longer. If she had, her gasping might have forced some air into her lungs and the goblet might not have slipped from her hand and shattered on the rock in the path to the servants' quarters. But she stumbled and fell, her foot getting tangled in a wild grapevine that had climbed and descended the stone wall next to the castle.

Two

That morning the snowflakes started high in the gray sky as tiny crystals with icy spikes. They crowded each other as they fell, swirling frantically, gathering half-frozen moisture on their descent, and finally plopping to earth, fat and wet.

It was too late in the year for snow; servants at the Castello di Gonzaga said that. So did the workers in the vineyard who only the week before had tended the vines in their shirt sleeves.

A few miles down the hill in the city of Ferrara, people who passed each other on the street remarked on the unseasonable weather. Some, the superstitious, prophesied disaster.

They thought of other years when the seasons had not arrived in their proper order, when spring had insinuated her way to the front of the line in January. In such a year grapes would appear on the vines and fresh beans in the market much too early, and the cuckoo, tentative at first, would grow boisterous and begin its call. Then winter, like a great hibernating bear, would blink in the sunshine and growl more ferociously than ever.

"Remember 1976?" someone in Ferrara would ask. Heads would nod. People thought of how icicles hung from ripe tomatoes in the fields that April when an earthquake shook the town and rang the bells of the cathedral for the length of an "Ave Maria." Other stories would be dredged up, stories that were as much a part of the city and as old as the statue of Nicolo III who sat on horseback atop the protruding arch of the Palazzo del Municipio.

Inevitably someone would mention the plague that had decimated Ferrara centuries before. The sickness, the storyteller would say ominously, had been carried in by mild weather that turned vicious and froze the lakes. And someone else would add that the invading French Army of Charles VIII had crossed the Po wearing summer uniforms just after Christmas. It was documented. You could ask a scholar at the university and he would tell you it was written on parchment in the archives.

Now, in March, the wary took the mothballs out of the pockets of woolen coats and wondered what catastrophe lay ahead.

But there were those who enjoyed the unexpected change in the weather. In front of the Este Hotel, three boys, their unbuttoned jackets flapping in the wind, threw sloppy snowballs at each other for practice, waiting for a better target to present itself. They did not have to wait long. A black limousine with the words "Gonzaga Vineyards" written in gold script on the side suddenly appeared at the corner. The boys depleted their stockpiles gleefully, spattering the side of the slow-moving vehicle as it passed by on its way to Ferrara's main tourist attraction, the castle of the despotic d'Este dukes.

From inside the lobby of the Este Hotel, the doorman frowned at the boys and briefly considered going out to shoo them away. But the snow wouldn't last long, he thought, let them have their fun. Besides, he felt no obligation to defend Count Gonzaga's Mercedes against the children of Ferrara. Like many of the local residents, he considered the Gonzagas interlopers who had attained their exalted position in the community by highly questionable methods.

While the late-comers among the breakfast crowd were having a last cup of espresso in the dining room, the lobby was almost deserted and looked particularly cheerless. The single theme of decoration was a series of faded posters advertising a Vittorio de Sica motion picture. De Sica had used the Este Hotel as headquarters a number of years before when he was in Ferrara filming *The Garden of the Finzi-Continis*.

Upstairs, in room three-fifty-one, Andrea Perkins sat in a chintz-upholstered chair facing the window. She hugged her knees to her chest and dug her bare feet into the softness of the cushion, wrapping the edge of a green woolen robe around her ankles for warmth as she watched the limousine's progression through the town center. At the end of the street, the car turned left onto the still-serviceable drawbridge above the moat that surrounded the gloomy old castle of Ferrara.

"Geoffredo must be taking his guests on a tour of the city," Andrea said loudly enough to be heard above the splash of water in the bathroom basin. "The limo from the winery just went by."

Aldo Balzani turned off the faucet and leaned against the doorway, wiping a stray blob of shaving cream from behind his ear. "So the renowned Carlo Gonzaga and his entourage have arrived."

"Apparently."

From Andrea's chair near the window, the limo was plainly visible as it turned toward the front of the castle of

Ferrara, which had been built in the fourteenth century as the official home and fortification for the ruling Este family. The Gonzaga castle had served as a summer retreat.

Andrea would have recognized the limousine even without "Gonzaga Vineyards" written on the side. It was the only stretch Mercedes six-hundred in this part of Italy, and practically the first thing she had seen when she arrived in Ferrara several weeks before. She had been hired to restore a group of miniature paintings that were part of the Gonzaga fortune. When her train arrived from Florence the automobile had been waiting at the station. She was quickly whisked out of the city and up through the gently sloping hills where the Po dipped down at Bondeno. This was the site of the second castle built by the Estes. Its pastoral setting provided privacy, if not tranquillity. Nor was life more tranquil for the second owners of the castle, the Gonzagas, than it had been for the Estes.

Andrea's assignment, like so many of her others, had come at the suggestion of the curator of the famed Galleria dell' Accademia in Florence.

". . . though she was trained in America . . ." The curator always included this phrase in a written recommendation; almost as an apology, it seemed to Andrea. ". . . she has a fine appreciation of the art of the Italian Renaissance and her technique of restoration is as skillful as anyone in the profession today."

Granted, the curator was given to superlatives, but his opinion of Andrea's ability was shared by others in the art world.

The limousine had been at her disposal all during her stay, and she had used it most recently five days ago to return to the train station. This time, her destination was Milan. The occasion was to attend a performance of *Rigoletto* at La Scala. Not in the Teatro della Scala, where

Verdi's fame was established, but in the rehearsal hall. The opera was performed by a small traveling company made up primarily of expatriate Americans. Because of the illness of one of the baritones, the role of the second courtier, for three nights only, was sung by the man Andrea considered the most important person in her life, Captain of Detectives Aldo Balzani of the Florentine Police Department.

"I still don't understand why you had to come back to Ferrara." Balzani, with little wisps of steam from the shower still floating around his towel-clad body, wiped the moisture from the bathroom mirror and vigorously rubbed at his wet dark hair with a hand towel. He was angry. He had expected her to return to Florence with him.

"I have some finishing-up work to do on a few of the miniatures. And there's a faded fresco on the outside of the castle that Geoffredo asked me to restore."

"I'd think there'd be enough peeling pictures and fading frescoes in Florence to keep you busy for the next fifty years." Balzani made a slight attempt to keep the exasperation out of his voice but was not successful.

"I go where I'm hired." Andrea turned to read his face but all she could see from where she sat was the back of his head and the top of his shoulders. The reflection of his face was blurred in the smeared and steamy bathroom mirror. A little rivulet the towel had missed dripped from his hair down the back of his neck. Her instinct was to go blot it with her hand, but there was something defensive about the set of his shoulders.

Andrea and Balzani did not talk a great deal about their work. In the six months they had known each other, there had barely been enough time to talk about themselves. But lately, confining schedules and professional commitments had been intruding more and more often. The greater the pleasure they took in each other, the more difficult the separations, especially for Balzani who could not accept Andrea's preoccupation with a career.

Aldo Balzani had entered Andrea's life at the same time and as unexpectedly as the portrait of Michelangelo's David.

The world press had not known immediately of her discovery. But other interested—and dangerous—parties had. And when it became a matter for the police, it had been Captain Balzani who took charge.

Andrea had been surprised to find that the Florentine captain of detectives had been brought up in America. Though he had been born in Italy, Balzani had spent his school years in New Orleans. At first, Andrea had found his Louisiana accent annoying, but it had become the sound of stability and sanity by the time her examination of the portrait of David was completed.

The published account of the discovery had linked the words thoroughness and expertise with Andrea's name. And in one of the more florid accounts, she had been described as "a young American art expert with a face that Botticelli would have wanted to paint, and copper-colored hair that would have inspired Titian."

The result of all the publicity was that Andrea's time was now booked a year in advance.

She found herself giving preference to projects in Italy because of her interest in the art of the Italian Renaissance. But stronger than that was her interest in Aldo Balzani.

"Extra time, that's what you said. The job in Ferrara wasn't going to take long and we'd have all this extra time." Balzani stood in the doorway looking stern.

Andrea grinned and raised her arm as though delivering a proclamation. "We've just had five glorious unexpected days in Milan where a previously undiscovered baritone stole the thunder from all the other courtiers in *Rigoletto*."

Balzani almost allowed himself to smile.

He had belonged to the Opera Club at Louisiana State University, and had also been a starting linebacker for the football team. He made no apology for either.

"I didn't know about the fresco when I agreed to restore the miniatures." Andrea's voice was soft and placatory.

"How long is that going to take?"

"I'm not sure yet."

"Do you see a lot of him?"

"Who?"

"Geoffredo Gonzaga." It was not just that Balzani wanted to spend more time with Andrea. He wanted her to spend *less* time with Geoffredo Gonzaga. Geoffredo was a widower and probably the most eligible single man in the province of Romagna.

"He stops by to check my progress now and then." Andrea pulled the collar of her robe up closer around her neck and shifted in the chair, tucking her feet under her and turning back toward the window.

The limousine had come to a stop next to the Este castle. Several people got out and hunched against the snow, hurrying toward the imposing stone colonnade at the entrance.

At this distance, the figures were distinct enough to count—there were seven—but too far away to distinguish their faces. They moved together and seemed to be etched in charcoal against the background of the gray day. All except one, who wore an iridescent pink cap and ran ahead of the others.

"There are seven people." Andrea began to tick them off on her fingers. "There would be Carlo . . ."

"Have you ever met him?"

"No."

"Both of you living in New York . . . and his being an artist . . ."

"There are lots of artists in New York I haven't met. Besides, he does the Jackson Pollock–type things that I never got very involved with. One of those people must be Carlo . . ." Again, she started counting the visitors on her fingers. ". . . and Geoffredo said . . ."

Geoffredo again, Balzani thought darkly.

". . . that Carlo had invited his mother-in-law and father-in-law and his stepdaughter . . ."

"What about his wife?"

"She's dead. Killed in an automobile accident not long ago."

Andrea tried to decide who the other three people were. "Carlo and his wife's family are four, and I think Carlo's business manager was coming, and some other friend that Geoffredo didn't seem to want to talk very much about. That's six. The seventh must be either the manager of the winery, Lucio Trotti, if he got elected tour guide, or Geoffredo himself." Andrea watched the small group until the castle door closed behind them. Aldo Balzani watched Andrea.

She was the art expert, not he, but Balzani could not imagine anything more beautiful than the curve of her cheek in profile and the soft glow of her reddish hair in the pale mid-morning light. Her hair was uncommon in color and texture. His first waking sensation that morning was to feel its softness tangled in his fingers. When he turned and saw her sleeping beside him he had been filled with a tenderness he could not have expressed, nor probably even admit.

In sudden exasperation he wadded the hand towel he had been holding into a tight ball. And, by God, that was what he wanted *every* morning: to see her head on the pillow beside him!

Balzani threw the towel back into the bathroom with such force that it knocked his shaving kit off the sink and onto the floor with an audible thud.

"What was that?"

"Nothing. It's okay." He picked up the kit and tossed it into his suitcase near the bed, then began to busy himself with getting dressed.

Andrea pushed the room service cart with its jam-smeared plates, crumb-dusted tablecloth, and empty coffeepot away from her chair and crossed the cold tile floor to the carved armoire. Balzani stared inside its open door, imitating a man intent on packing. He needlessly set all the wire hangers clattering as he took out his two shirts that hung there. Andrea stood silently for a moment, warming one bare foot on top of the other as she watched him toss the shirt he had worn yesterday toward the suitcase and thrust his arms into the sleeves of the fresh one.

"You're beginning to act like an Italian," she said.

"I am an Italian."

"An Italian husband, then."

"Would that be so bad?" Balzani pulled the edges of his shirt together and began buttoning it from the bottom up.

"Not for the husband."

"You love someone . . . you get married, that's all. It's just something that caught on in Italy—other places, too, I understand." Balzani took a blue and white striped tie from a peg inside the armoire and draped it around his neck. He flipped the ends across each other with the quick, sure movements of a magician rolling a coin across his knuckles.

"I love you," Andrea said matter-of-factly.

". . . and when you're married, you live together, like

15

Uncle Alfredo and his wife. They've been married thirty-five years."

Uncle Alfredo's wife: that was the woman's name. After thirty-five years of marriage, Andrea thought, her name is Uncle Alfredo's wife.

"Andrea." Balzani pushed the knot of his tie up to the top of his collar. "I don't think I'm being medieval, I don't mean to be. I like getting your calls from London or Madrid or wherever the hell you happen to be preserving the art of antiquity for the yet unborn generations. It's all very noble. It's a high calling." His voice grew softer and the words came faster. "Hell, I know you're talented. I'm not discounting your talent or the amount of work it takes." He stuffed his shirt into his trousers and threaded a black leather belt through the loops. "It's just that right now, right *then* when I'm talking to you on the phone from God knows where," he stopped a moment, then said, "I want to kiss your neck, or take hold of your hand. And we can't manage that over long distance, can we?"

He let his arms drop to his sides and looked at her with an honesty of emotion that cut through superfluous words. If Shakespeare's eyes had been as convincing as Balzani's, Andrea often had thought, he might never have bothered to write the sonnets.

"It's just that I want to be with you more," he said. "I want to see you every day."

He did not touch her with his hands. They stayed at his side. If she had moved toward him, even leaned forward to take a step, he would have reached out and held her tight against his chest.

If he had reached out, she would not have been able to leave.

But the combination of need and pride in both of them turned caustic and distilled into inertia. The moment of silence grew too heavy and the bridge of compromise collapsed under its weight.

Balzani's glance shifted from Andrea's face back to his suitcase. "It's late," he said. "I have a train to catch."

Andrea stared down at the cold tile floor that suddenly looked blurry. She bunched the lapels of her robe together and held them close to her chest as she felt under the corner of the bed for her scuffs with one bare foot. "You can't stay for Geoffredo's reception this evening?"

"No. I have to get back to Florence."

"I understand. I understand if you have work to do." If Balzani recognized the irony of her words, he did not show it. "I have some research to do myself," Andrea said.

Three

Andrea dressed quickly in jeans and a plaid shirt and left the room only minutes after the elevator door closed behind Aldo Balzani.

Work, she decided, was the best remedy for the emptiness she felt. There was a painting she needed to examine at the Este castle, then she would spend the rest of the day scraping and replastering the Gonzaga fresco. With luck, by evening she would be too tired to think of anything at all.

Downstairs, she slipped into her raincoat, buttoning and belting it as the doorman carried her suitcase out through the lobby. He offered to find a cab for her.

"No thank you," she said, "but could you arrange to have someone meet me later at the Este castle?"

The snow was not as heavy now as it had been an hour before. Most of it that reached the sidewalk melted immediately or stuck to the dirty clumps of slush at the base of the buildings and in the gutters.

"Sì, signorina. The driver will take you there and wait for you."

"I'd rather walk." She gave the doorman a generous tip.

"But I'll need a taxi to go back to the Gonzaga castle. Send someone up with my suitcase in about an hour."

The doorman pocketed the tip before saying, "The Gonzaga limousine is already there. Perhaps you would prefer to ride back in it?"

"No. I would prefer a taxi." Andrea did not intend to make explanations to the doorman. The truth was, she did not want to share the limousine with Geoffredo Gonzaga's guests. She was in no mood to talk with anyone just now. Tonight would be soon enough to meet Geoffredo's brother Carlo and his friends from New York.

"Sì, signorina, in one hour a taxi will come for you."

Andrea started the uphill climb toward the castle. Since she had been a child, whenever she did not care for her own company, she pretended she was someone else. Alice in Wonderland had been her first other self. In her teens, Alice was replaced by Mary Cassat and later by any of the Brontë sisters, since she could never keep them straight, anyway.

Now, she imagined herself to be the future Duchess of Este, the young woman whose bridal procession was depicted in the fresco Andrea had been commissioned to restore. As she came nearer the formidable castle, she tried to picture the city as the Duchess had seen it for the first time almost five hundred years ago.

Sketching in her mind a curious crowd lining the street for a glimpse of Alfonso d'Este's bride, Andrea added the sound of cheering voices and the colors of streaming banners.

"She pleased the people so greatly that they are perfectly satisfied with her." Andrea had read the line in a journal of the period. It had surprised her. The delight of the townfolk with their new duchess seemed inconsistent with the lady's reputation.

Further research convinced Andrea that the people of Ferrara had been right in their first favorable impression. When the duchess was called upon to rule in her husband's absence, she was fair and compassionate. So how had this woman gained a reputation as one of history's vilest females?

The Duke of Este was reputed to have been a cruel, philandering scoundrel. His reputation was already well established by the time the wedding took place. First-hand accounts of beheadings, hangings, imprisonments, even the blinding and torture of his own brother still exist for the interested to read. But with no such evidence it was the Duchess of Este who gained the lasting reputation as the epitome of evil. Andrea refused to believe it.

The deeper she dug into the archives of the University of Ferrara where the written accounts of that period were preserved, the more she was convinced that the real target for defamation was the father of the duchess. He was a powerful man with many enemies. The scurrilous stories concerning the young woman's virtue were told by those who hoped to harm the father through the daughter. The lady had been maligned.

Andrea crossed the bridge that spanned the moat where a thin layer of ice covered the shallow water.

The Gonzaga limousine was the only automobile in the parking lot. The chilling wind and wet snow were enough to discourage most sightseers. But Ferrara was never among the great tourist attractions of Italy, even in the best of weather. It was not well-located to be included on a package tour of Florence, Venice, and Rome.

Andrea entered the first anteroom and stood in a shadowed alcove near the door for a moment, listening and trying to determine where the tour guide and Geoffredo's guests were.

"Now we see the dungeon where Duke Alfonso d'Este imprisoned his enemies." The guard's voice, punctuated by the sound of prison keys being dramatically clanked together, bounced against the sheer stone walls of the barren dining hall and echoed back toward the entrance.

The tour must have started on the second floor and was working its way down, Andrea thought. Good. She was going the opposite way. Her rubber-soled sneakers made no sound as she ran up the marble steps toward the living quarters of the Estes. That was where the painting was that she had come to see. She wanted to compare the portrait of the duchess with the face on the fresco she had been commissioned to restore.

She heard the creak of ancient hinges as the foot-thick door that led down to the dungeon swung open. The guard's voice faded as the group descended into the depths of the castle.

After first taking a wrong turn, she found the room she was looking for. It was identified by a bronze plaque as the bridal chamber of the Duke and Duchess of Este. There was an additional handwritten notation on a three-by-five card that the furniture was the original but that the carpet and prominent fabrics had been replaced, duplicating the original. The walls were hung with deep brown velvet, as much for warmth as decoration, she thought, shivering in the doorway. Drapes of the same depressing color hung from the high ceiling to the floor and blocked out most of the gray daylight that seeped through the windows. Andrea could recognize only outlines of furniture. A huge bed stood on an elevated pedestal, a writing desk and a straight-backed chair were between two windows, and a cluster of couches and tables were grouped against the far wall.

She breathed in the melancholy silence with the mustiness of the air.

What had the new Duchess of Este felt when she first saw this room?

She had grown up among the privileged of Rome in an atmosphere of opulence and gaiety. Then, as the betrothed of the Duke of Este she had traveled by carriage for days to reach this austere northern city leaving her friends, her family, her home behind her. When she saw this dismal castle fear must have overwhelmed her.

Why has my father sent me here alone to live among strangers?

Could a twenty-year-old bride who had met her husband for the first time that day have felt anything else?

Can I survive? How can I survive?

Had the answer she had given herself been, *Endure. Insulate your soul within yourself and endure.*

Or had it been, *Prevail: Survive by whatever means.*

Even if the last were true, it did not necessarily follow that the young woman was innately wicked. She was her father's pawn.

Andrea felt uneasy. Maybe it was not wise to try to go so far inside the mind of another person. She felt displaced, disoriented. Taking a step backward, she bumped against the door. Her heel struck and dislodged the wooden wedge that held it open, and the door instantly swung closed, shutting out even the dim light from the hallway. Something near panic burned in her throat.

She reached for the handle but could not find it. When she tried to turn, she found she could not move. Something held her from behind. She lurched forward, twisting her body to the side, intent on pounding on the door with her fist. It was then she realized what had happened. The tail of her raincoat had caught and meshed in the closed hinge.

The feeling of relief made her tremble. Still, she was caught. She swept her hand up and down against the wide wooden surface, but the latch was out of reach. Again, she thought of pounding on the door, but realized the group in the dungeon would never hear her.

Don't be an idiot, she said to herself. Just take your coat off! What is there to get panicked about?

As quickly as she could, she undid the buttons and belt, slipped out of her captured coat and opened the door.

Harmless as the incident had been, the fear had been real. It had crackled in the room through the dark curtains, over the wide bed, up the walls and across the ceiling, springing at her fresh and electric. It had not been generated in her mind alone.

It had been shared. It was as though she had experienced it through someone else. The moment, the emotion had belonged not only to Andrea, but to the Duchess of Este, Lucrezia Borgia.

Four

The Este castle in Ferrara was maintained as a museum by the state. The second castle that had been Lucrezia's summer retreat on the Po near Bondeno was now the property of Geoffredo Gonzaga.

The sprawling, quarry-stone edifice had been owned by the family of Geoffredo and his brother Carlo Gonzaga for the past three hundred years. But there were still those who questioned the Gonzagas' right of ownership. There were still whispered stories of chicanery.

The Gonzagas themselves always maintained that the transfer of title was strictly honest. The castle and the vineyards had been the stakes in a legitimate bet. A Gonzaga forebear won them in a card game from a member of the ruling Este family of Ferrara. On that night when the playing cards, the *tarocchi*, were dealt, luck deserted the Estes, and sat with the Gonzagas.

The castle was built in the second year of the sixteenth century by Alfonso d'Este for his bride, Lucrezia Borgia.

As was customary, the marriage had been arranged by the fathers of the bride and groom. The young couple had never met before their wedding day. Lucrezia had been

25

accepted as a suitable daughter-in-law by Alfonso's father, Duke Ercole Este of Ferrara, though her reputation, even then, was more than a little unsavory.

She had been married twice before. The first marriage ended in an annulment when her young husband fell out of favor with Lucrezia's father. A bribe of thirty-one thousand ducats was offered to the bridegroom's father if he would persuade his son to dissolve the marriage. And though the young man had been Lucrezia's husband for three years, he agreed, under threat and duress, to sign a statement that he had never "known" his wife: *quod non cognoverim Lucrezia.* The document was witnessed and recorded. Once Lucrezia was released from the marriage, she was officially returned to the status of virgin, *virgae intactae.* And within a year her father had arranged for her to be a bride for the second time.

The fate of husband number two was worse than that of the first bridegroom. The young man Lucrezia's father chose the second time died under questionable circumstances. No charges were ever made, no murderer ever found, but he met death in his bedroom in the presence of his wife. The official report read: "From the wound that had been inflicted in his head, blood flowed copiously and thus he breathed his last." Lucrezia was said to have grieved "mightily." Husband number two, it is believed, was the love of her life, but he unfortunately fell out of favor with her father and her brother Cesare.

As if her past matrimonial record were not enough to discourage a third husband, there was the question of parentage. Lucrezia was known to have been born out of wedlock. Her father never married the woman who bore him three children.

All of this part of Lucrezia Borgia's history was fact. There were also the rumors.

26

The accusation most often repeated was of incest. It was said that the debauchery involved not only Lucrezia and her father but also Lucrezia and her brother Cesare. There were other whispered stories that the young woman was handy with poison, and that a number of Lucrezia's enemies had not survived dinner parties given in their honor.

Naturally, all of this gave the Duke of Ferrara pause. He carefully considered the reputation of this blond creature who was still only twenty years old before agreeing that his son should become husband number three. But ultimately the duke was persuaded. He recognized that Lucrezia had one virtue that outweighed all the real and rumored vices: her father was the most powerful man in Rome, perhaps in the whole world. Lucrezia, though illegitimate, was the acknowledged daughter of the vicar of Christ, the spiritual leader of all Christendom; her doting father was Pope Alexander VI.

In fairness to the tainted name of Borgia, it is well to be reminded that the Este family history was not without its own stain.

Alfonso Este, Lucrezia's third husband-to-be, had been married before. His wife had died in childbirth. But far from being a solicitous husband, Alfonso had spent more time in brothels than in the arms of his wife. And as the wages for his sin he contracted what the fifteenth-century Italians called the "French disease," and the fifteenth-century French called the "Italian disease."

Nor was Alfonso the only Este to fall from grace. Dante, in his *Divine Comedy*, assigned some of Alfonso's relatives to everlasting damnation. In the poet's allegorical journey through hell, he reported that he came upon the fourth Marchese of Ferrara in the river of boiling blood where fierce centaurs hunt the damned souls of tyrants and murderers. Dante consigned another Este from Milan to the

Evil Pits of seducers of women for making Dante's sister "do the Marchese's will."

Geoffredo and Carlo Gonzaga had grown up hearing twentieth-century versions of the history of the Castello di Gonzaga. They were no more impressed than any other boys whose preteen interests were being the fastest runner, having the shiniest bicycle, or growing the tallest. And in adolescence and young manhood, their greatest concerns were their individual prospects for becoming rich and famous, and the beauty of the girls they attracted.

Some artifacts from the castle's colorful past survived the centuries. A single red goblet of Venetian glass that bore the crest of the Borgias (a golden bull in a field of wheat) had sat on the top shelf of an antique cabinet in the hallway next to the kitchen for as long as anyone could remember. And there was a shopping list for silk and ribbons said to have been written by Lucrezia. It was preserved in a safe behind a portrait of an eighteenth-century Gonzaga count. Also in the safe were a few unidentified pieces of jewelry and a deck of paper *tarocchi*, or playing cards.

The *tarocchi* were made of cardboard and backed with a thin sheet of filigreed ivory. The figure or design on each card was exquisitely hand-painted. The artist was said to have been Bonifacio Bembo, the most famous of the Renaissance miniaturists. The cards had survived because of the foresight of some previous family member in protecting them from mildew and strong light.

The castle held a few sturdier reminders of the past: a writing desk, a silver-backed hairbrush, and a wine barrel with the date 1473 carved in its side along with the initials of some long-forgotten *celleraro*, a worker in the winery. But just as someone who has grown up at the foot of the Matterhorn does not rise every morning and say "Ah, look at that magnificent mountain!" the Gonzaga brothers rarely commented on the backdrop of their own past.

Carlo was the first to remember the *tarocchi*.

A few months before his present visit to Italy, Carlo wrote to his brother inquiring about the condition of the playing cards. He suggested that if it seemed feasible, they should be restored.

Though Geoffredo knew that the word *tarocchi* translated in English was tarot, he had no knowledge of Carlo's new interest in the occult, and assumed that his brother's interest was purely artistic.

His own sudden enthusiasm for the project was vindication. As head of the house of Gonzaga and a resident of Ferrara, Geoffredo continued to hear the old stories that the castle and vineyards had been won in an unfair card game. Legends, especially those of evil-doing, did not die easily in Italy, and since many of the citizens of Ferrara claimed kinship with the Este family (either legitimately or on the wrong side of the blanket) there were periodic rumblings that "this one" or "that one" was the rightful heir to the castle and vineyards. The claims, over the years, had grown at about the same ratio as had the passenger list of the Mayflower in America. Not that it mattered legally after more than three hundred years, but Geoffredo would be glad to put the story to rest once and for all.

At the recommendation of Vittorio Sassetti, the curator of the Galleria dell' Accademia in Florence, Geoffredo hired Andrea Perkins to restore the *tarocchi*. Andrea was able to establish that Bonifacio Bembo was indeed the artist. Through a microscopic examination of the vine design that delicately outlined the face of each card, she proved it conclusively. The artist had signed his name in script on each one in what appeared at first to be merely a design of the interlinking tendrils of the grapevines.

Of more interest to Geoffredo Gonzaga was Andrea's

discovery that none of the *tarocchi* was illegally marked. If, indeed, these were the cards used in that long-ago game, there was nothing to indicate that the winner had an unfair advantage, at least as far as an illegal deck was concerned. But the problem was that, from a deck of fifty-three cards, two were missing.

Five

Andrea found the latch and pushed the door open, then tugged at the tail of her raincoat to free it from the hinge. With the light from the hallway streaming inside, the bridal chamber of the Este castle did not look quite so forbidding. Still, she was glad to see a notice tacked to the outside wall that she had not read earlier telling visitors that the portrait of Lucrezia she had come to see was now on display in the first-floor library.

As she hurried back down the stairs she heard the crunch of tires on gravel, and glanced through a Gothic window opposite the stairwell to see the Gonzaga limousine turn toward the moat and leave fresh tracks in the snow as it crossed the bridge.

The library in the castle of Ferrara had a warmth that was lacking in the rest of the austere fortress. There were three walls of shelves stacked with books and a comfortable fire crackling away in the mammoth fireplace. Above the stone mantel was the portrait of Lucrezia. It was not an original, but a copy of the fresco on a wall of the papal chamber in the vatican. The artist, Pinturicchio, had titled it *The Disputation of Saint Catherine,* and depicted a sweet-faced and innocent Lucrezia as the saint.

In a small souvenir shop just inside the entry Andrea bought a set of six thirty-five millimeter color slides featuring the high points of a visit to Ferrara: the castle, the Este Hotel, the statue of Nicolo III on his horse, one of the world's first cannons developed by Alfonso d'Este (his contribution to mankind), the Gothic cathedral with the Virgin enthroned above the west door, and the portrait of Lucrezia.

The taxi Andrea had tipped the doorman at the Este Hotel to order was predictably late, by a full thirty minutes. It did not matter a great deal as far as delaying the repair to the fresco was concerned. It would be so cold on the scaffold the plaster would freeze as soon as she mixed it. But a few of the *tarocchi* still needed some attention.

By the time the taxi had left the city and turned onto the road to Bondeno, Andrea had forgotten her earlier eerie experience in the bridal chamber and was mentally cataloging the work that remained to be done at the Gonzaga castle.

Geoffredo Gonzaga had spent the last several hours in his office and had not known when the limousine returned. Now he hurried from the Gonzaga winery to the castle.

The walkway between the two was covered by an arched canopy of green canvas with gold "G" 's stenciled on every fourth scallop of the overhang. The protected sidewalk had remained dry during the morning's snow flurries, but the road that ran alongside was churned into rutted mud by the trucks from the vineyards.

Just as Geoffredo reached the service wing of the castle an empty flatbed diesel on its way to the loading dock behind the bottling room drove past, sending up a spray of brown muck. Geoffredo dodged out of the way of the flying mud, then checked to make sure none had landed on his Briani suit. Satisfied, he entered the kitchen and closed the door behind him.

The chef, or *direttore* of food and wine, as he referred to himself in the daily written instructions to the staff, turned from stirring a deep aluminum pot on the stove. "Buon giorno, Signore Gonzaga."

Geoffredo nodded in response. "Have my brother Carlo and the others returned?"

"They finished luncheon about fifteen minutes ago." The chef wiped his hands on his white apron. "My capelletti was well received." The chef was justly proud of his pasta stuffed with a sweetish pumpkin mixture. "Allow me to prepare a plate for you."

Geoffredo held up a hand in protest, "No, no." He had been watching his diet lately. His weight was not really a problem, except for a slight bulge around the waist, and that did not show when he kept his jacket buttoned. The physical changes he had feared as he neared his fiftieth birthday were, for Geoffredo, minimal.

"Some fresh marinated hearts of artichoke . . ."

"Nothing for me now." Geoffredo started toward the hallway and the back stairs to his apartment when he noticed the six bottles of Sangiovese di Romagna neatly lined up on the serving area of the cabinet like so many pins in a bowling alley. "What is that?"

"Signore?" The chef was startled by the anger in Geoffredo's voice.

"Did you serve Sangiovese at luncheon?"

"With capelletti? Never!" The chef was offended at the suggestion that he could make such a mistake. "Signore Carlo and his friends drank Montuni del Reno."

"The Sangiovese is to be served with dinner!"

"The wine was placed here only in preparation for this evening," the chef insisted.

"See that it's not disturbed." Geoffredo started for the stairs again. "I'll decant it myself at the proper time."

Pausing at the stove, Geoffredo peered into the large aluminum pan, where a clear, simmering liquid turned and swirled around wide strips of something white. "And what is this? Some new specialty?" Geoffredo was prepared to offer a placating compliment.

"It is rags, signore," the chef sniffed, not yet willing to forget the injustice.

"Rags?"

"For Signorina Perkins. She asked me to boil white linen rags. To make paper, she said."

"I understand," Geoffredo said, though he did not. But if the chef had told him that Andrea had asked for lizards' tongues or black toadstools, his response would have been the same. Her work was a mystery to him, but the results were amazing. He had instructed the staff to cooperate with her whenever possible, and if she needed white linen rags, she would have them. "Is she back yet?"

"I have not seen her, signore."

"When she comes in, ask if she needs anything special for her presentation this evening."

"We discussed it before she left." Defensively the chef began to list the preparations that had already been made for the reception and dinner party. "Chairs have been arranged in the salon as she suggested. The table in the dining room has been set for eleven . . ."

"Ten. There will be ten guests."

"And yourself, signore." The chef flavored his words with a touch of smugness as subtle as the garlic in his capelletti. "Eleven."

"Of course, eleven." Geoffredo gave the chef a friendly thump on the back with his open palm. "I'll be in my apartment if anyone needs me."

When he was gone, the chef glanced with relief at the cabinet where the Sangiovese stood. Thank heaven he had recorked the bottle he found open and placed it behind the others so the neck with the missing lead seal did not show.

Imagine Signore Gonzaga asking if he had served it with luncheon! An Este would never have made such an accusation.

The chef prided himself on knowing the wine cellar as well as, if not better, than anyone. He knew the shapes of the bottles, the labels they bore, the year of the vintage and its color: everything, in fact, but the taste. His responsibility was to serve the right wine, not drink it. Well, yes, occasionally, he surreptitiously drank the remains of a half-full glass returned from the table, or finished off a bottle that had not been drained. Where was the harm? It only served to strengthen his own preference for Chianti.

He picked up the opened bottle of Sangiovese and made a mental note to replace it with another one from the cellar. Wait until he caught up with whoever was responsible! He could not believe anyone on his staff would do such a thing. It must have been the girl from the temporary service. One could never depend on temporary help to do the right thing.

There were already two reasons for the reception. One was the return of Geoffredo's brother Carlo from New York. The other was the unveiling of the set of newly restored fifteenth-century *tarocchi* miniature watercolors. And if the day progressed as Geoffredo planned, there would be an even happier event to celebrate. The reception would be an excellent time to announce plans for his personal future and, of course, that of the signorina whom he was going to ask to share it.

It was news of the *tarocchi,* not brotherly love, that had brought Carlo back to Italy. Geoffredo knew that. Not that there was any open animosity between the two. They simply had gone their separate ways.

When first their mother and then their father died, Geoffredo had stayed in Ferrara. As the oldest son, he inherited the title of Count and the presidency of the Gonzaga winery. Carlo had emigrated to New York and become, by his own account, a financial and critical success as a painter. His huge "action" paintings, as he called them, graced the walls of well-to-do Americans who were fanciers of abstract expressionism but not quite wealthy enough to afford an original canvas by Jackson Pollock.

Geoffredo respected his brother's success, if not his talent.

Too bad, Geoffredo thought for the thousandth time, that the Gonzaga vineyards could not turn such a profit with so little effort. But life would improve. By tomorrow he hoped to be richer in more than just money.

Geoffredo took the last of the stairs to his third-floor apartment. As always, he felt awkward to be entering it alone. The rooms were designed to be used by a man and his wife.

The armoire had been handcrafted by some long-forgotten artisan to accommodate both male and female wardrobes. The bed, too, was meant to be shared. Its mahogany posts with their carved spiraling design of vines and cupids pointed to a ceiling fresco of an enraptured Jupiter and Juno in pastel shades of pinks and golds and blues.

It was time, again, to put the apartment to the use for which it had been intended.

Geoffredo frowned. There was one difficulty. It would not be easy to explain his decision to remarry Caterina.

Caterina would be a problem. But in the end, he felt sure she would understand. They had always had an understanding. She could not share his life at the castle or give him children. There had never been any question of that. Caterina already had a husband.

Geoffredo turned toward the gilt mirror and rehearsed his performance for the evening. He would personally pour the wine. And when all the glasses were filled, he would greet his guests and make his announcement. Lifting an imaginary glass to his reflection he recited the toast he would make with the Sangiovese di Romagna.

Carlo Gonzaga had taken his old room directly beneath Geoffredo's apartment. Sammy Hirschfeld, Carlo's agent and business manager, had been given the room on the left; Fletcher Kimball, the artist's personal astrologer, the one on the right.

Without looking up from the painting he was studying on his easel, Carlo said to Sammy Hirschfeld who stood in the connecting doorway, "Geoffredo is planning to get married." The artist flourished a long thin paintbrush in the air as though he were unfurling a flag. For some time his brother had been hinting that he might consider marriage again. Then in his last letter he mentioned a likely candidate. "He told me this morning."

"What's so extraordinary about that?" Hirschfeld made a habitual attempt to flatten his sparse hair that sprang back like fine uncoiling wire the moment his hands were lifted.

The folding table set up next to the easel was in its usual state of disarray, stacked with tubes of pigment, a variety of brushes, a pitcher of water, and an untidy stack of periodicals devoted to news of the art world. In one of them, a back issue of *American Art Review*, Carlo had been described as "... a young lion with flying black mane and the eyes of a Halloween cat."

In the corner of the room, on the floor, Fletcher Kimball, the astrologer, sat with his thin legs intertwined like knotted ropes, his head bent over a pack of cards spread out in front of him.

Sammy Hirschfeld did not acknowledge Fletcher Kimball's presence. From their first meeting several months before, the two men had made their distrust of each other apparent.

"Geoffredo's sudden interest in matrimony is extraordinary only in its timing. He's been a widower for almost ten years now." Carlo stepped back a moment, pulling on his underlip as he studied the painting in front of him. "I thought he was enjoying his status of eligible widowerhood. The winery and *la bella* Caterina seemed to keep him busy enough."

"Maybe it's a delayed case of sibling rivalry," Sammy Hirschfeld said. "He could be going for your record."

"My record? I wouldn't think four marriages constituted a record." If the tone of Carlo's voice could have been painted, it would have been the same shade of glacial blue that coated his paintbrush.

Watch it, Sammy Hirschfeld admonished himself. I should not have said that. There had been four marriages, yes, but only three divorces. Not bad considering some of the artists the Hirschfeld Agency represented. And the automobile accident that had killed Carlo's last wife was scarcely more than six months past.

To change the subject, Sammy Hirschfeld mentally sifted through a number of topics that might fall on neutral ground when he stumbled upon one that truly astonished him: the painting his client was working on at the easel.

That Carlo was using an easel at all was unique, and the fact that the painting was a delicate watercolor miniature was astounding. A miniature! A watercolor miniature, at that, when his reputation had been built on paintings the size of small billboards and done in acrylic paint.

Back in New York, part of Sammy Hirschfeld's sales technique on his client's behalf had been to invite a potential buyer to Carlo's studio to see the artist at work. It was rather like watching a primo ballet dancer without the music.

Carlo's usual procedure was to spread a gigantic canvas out flat on a platform on the floor. The background color was "laid-on" with a long-handled brush that looked like a janitor's broom. When that was dry, Carlo walked, barefoot, across the canvas with a can of paint in one hand. Sometimes he let the acrylic drip from a large hog-bristle brush in a seemingly random pattern, sometimes he splashed the pigment directly from the can onto the canvas. As unstructured as the entire performance seemed, the result was an amazing transference of energy from the artist to the painting.

The actual physical process—Carlo's pirouetting steps, his stretching strides, his long arms dipping and bending and reaching as he splattered the paint—all this was the prime instrument of his expression. And his virtuoso performance, Sammy Hirschfeld thought grimly, was what sold his paintings.

Hirschfeld glanced at his client as though at a stranger. Usually when he was working, Carlo's attitude was of childlike abandon. Now his body was taut, as though it took all his muscular coordination to wield the small squirrel-hair brush between his thumb and forefinger in a manner that was as gentle as the subject of the painting.

Sammy Hirschfeld pulled a pair of half-glasses from his pocket and leaned closer to examine the tiny brushstrokes applied to the cardboard miniature. His voice was genuinely surprised, but he tried to sound enthusiastic. "What's this?"

"A portrait."

"Yes, I see."

"Something different."

"Yes. Yes it is."

It was a portrait of a young woman, so far faceless, in a patterned black dress. Her light-colored hair flowed in serpentine strands to her waist. Her hands were held in front of her chest with the fingers barely touching in a style often seen in Renaissance portraiture. It was lovely. It was charming. But from abstract expressionism to miniatures—Carlo's admirers would never let him get away with it!

"It *is* something different," Hirschfeld said.

"It's time. I'm bored with the other."

"But the market for watercolors isn't exactly strong—" Sammy Hirschfeld cautioned himself and stopped midsentence. Maybe a change in style was exactly what was needed. Carlo's paintings had not been selling well lately. The last one had been purchased to hang in the reception room of a Fifth Avenue dentist. His client's personal popularity was waning, too. He seldom was photographed at gallery openings or posh benefits anymore. Sammy knew that Carlo worried about it. Not long ago he had remarked that it seemed the "fifteen minutes of celebrity" Andy Warhol said was allotted to every person had already gone by for him. Then Carlo had thrown a paintbrush against the wall and said, "God! I wish *I* had said that. That line did as much to make Warhol famous as his soup cans."

Hold on a second, Sammy Hirschfeld reasoned with himself, consider miniatures for a moment. They were sometimes successful. Some miniatures sold very well. Especially those with intrinsic value—the ones painted on jade, or antique ivory, or enameled gold. Hirschfeld had once sold a miniature portrait of a poodle painted on an onyx broach for an excellent price. Of course, it had been commissioned by the dog's owner. But still, miniatures could be successful.

Hirschfeld looked closely at Carlo's painting again, first with his glasses, then without. The subject was a young woman of the Italian Renaissance. Italian Renaissance paintings were popular. There would always be a buyer for a true Renaissance painting, especially if there was an identifiable signature and the artist was listed as one of the leaders of the period, or even a known student of one of the masters. But Sammy Hirschfeld's nervousness crept back with renewed vigor. Both his hands flew to the top of his head to plaster down his springy hair. Okay, he thought, miniatures—maybe. *If* they had intrinsic value. Renaissance portraits—perhaps. But there was one thing Sammy Hirschfeld knew for sure. The was *no* market for Renaissance miniatures painted in watercolors on cardboard by a living artist!

"That's a charming little picture." Sammy hoped his voice sounded slightly enthusiastic—but only slightly. He did not want to encourage the artist. "Did you work in watercolors when you studied in Florence?"

"Some." Carlo stepped back to appraise his effort, squinting his green eyes in concentration.

"It's interesting to see you experimenting with tech-

41

nique." Sammy's voice had risen in pitch. "I suppose that being back in Italy, you feel a need to review some of the basics."

"No." Carlo looked directly at his agent. "I felt . . . compelled to paint it." If his face had an identifiable expression, it was—peaceful.

"Can't you see what happened, Sammy?" Fletcher Kimball spoke for the first time since Sammy Hirschfeld had entered the room. "Carlo is being 'other' directed."

"Oh, God! What the hell does that mean, 'other' directed?" Sammy asked the question of Carlo, but it was Fletcher Kimball who answered.

"It's quite simple. Some inner force, some previous self is guiding his hands."

Sammy felt like screaming. So this was all Fletcher Kimball's doing. Kimball with his mumbo jumbo, his cards and past-life regressions, had convinced Carlo of God knew what!

The room was silent for a moment. Hirschfeld fumed. Carlo painted. Kimball shuffled the deck of cards again, and was the first to speak.

"Carlo," the astrologer said, rising from the lotus position without touching his hands to the floor. "This deck doesn't seem to tell me anything significant. The cards your brother promised to show us may give a truer reading." Kimball bent at the waist and deftly scooped up the deck with one hand. "The only thing that seems certain is that there definitely is a restless presence in this castle."

"Why are you so restless?" Murray Eastman, in the room across from Carlo's, watched his wife pull back the curtain and stare down into the courtyard for at least the tenth time in the last hour. "Harriet, you can't watch Tess every second."

"You act as though I'm spying on her." Harriet sounded indignant. "Where is she?"

"Probably still in the winery."

"Since when has Tess been interested in touring a winery?"

Since she met the manager of the Gonzaga winery who looks like Sylvester Stallone with a mustache, Murray Eastman thought.

"She's paying too much attention to that Lucio . . ."

"Trotti." No more than to any man who was reasonably attractive. Men seemed to be their granddaughter's only interest. "Lucio Trotti."

"I don't like him."

"He's all right." Murray had found Trotti quite agreeable and cooperative when they toured the vineyards and aging cellars. True, Murray's interest in wineries was keener than most. It was his business. Only Heublein and Seagram imported more French and Italian wines to the United States than the Murray Eastman Company.

"She needs supervision. She never *did* have much, and now there won't be any at all," Harriet said.

Murray Eastman shook his head sadly. He watched his wife at the window and studied the new bulges in her jersey dress. She must have gained twenty pounds in the last six months. Solace, for her, seemed linked somehow with food, and more and more often—vodka. Grief took different forms for different people. Murray would have liked to share his. But whenever he said their daughter's name his wife would leave the room, and the next time he saw her she would have a drink in her hand. All Harriet seemed to be interested in now was their granddaughter, Tess.

"Tess is of age. There's not much supervision anyone can give her anymore," Murray said.

"How can eighteen be considered 'of age'?"

Murray went to the window where his wife was standing and put his arm loosely around her shoulder. "Harriet, Tess is not our responsibility."

Harriet's back stiffened. If Tess would only come and live with them, it would be much better for everyone. Harriet had made mistakes with her daughter; she would admit that. Every mother makes mistakes. But she had learned from hers. And if she had the chance, she would do things differently with Tess.

Harriet bit into her lip to stop it from trembling. Of all nature's cruelties, the cruelest thing of all must be to outlive your young.

God, she wished she had a drink! But at the moment it was not worth the worried look that would appear on Murray's face when she asked him to fix her one.

The car crash that had killed her daughter would never be forgotten by Harriet Eastman. Why had Carlo Gonzaga been the one to escape unharmed? Harriet would never forgive her son-in-law, never stop blaming him, though the police and the insurance company were satisfied that the accident had been unavoidable.

Harriet patted Murray's hand that was resting on her shoulder. He tried, she knew, but nothing he said really seemed to help. "Has Tess told you her latest plan?"

"No, what?"

"She wants to go back to New York and live in the apartment with Carlo."

"It's just talk." Murray tried to make the whole idea sound ridiculous. He even forced a convincing laugh. "She'll end up going back to school."

"It just wouldn't be proper! With his reputation and her age. It would be different if he were her *real* father."

Legally, he was—though Murray did not point that out. Tess had been twelve when Carlo and their daughter married. The adoption had been meant as an anchor, the agreement a wealthy older woman had extracted from a young husband she did not trust.

"There. There she is!" Harriet let the curtain fall closed except for an inch-wide opening she peered through. "The clothes she wears—or *doesn't* wear! It's starting to snow again and she's out there without a jacket, just a tight sweater. You'd think she was the only female who'd ever developed breasts." Harriet pulled her shoulders straight in faint surprise. She had long ago forgotten the possible attractions of her own.

Murray pretended not to notice. Tess, he thought, had not had her impressive bustline long enough to get used to it.

"It's shameful the way she throws herself at men," Harriet said. "They don't even have to be able to speak the same language!"

"Grazie, Signorina Teseo." Lucio Trotti closed and locked the door to the business office and thanked Tess again for allowing him to take her on a tour of the Gonzaga winery.

"I like the way you say my name. Carlo calls me Teseo, too. It's so much nicer than . . . Tess."

"Signorina, *Tess*." Lucio Trotti had not understood and thought she was correcting him.

"No, no. I *like* having you call me Teseo." Tess laughed and let her long smooth fingers brush across the sleeve of Lucio's coveralls.

"Teseo." He let the sibilant simmer between his lips.

Tess was the product of multivitamins and several generations of intermingling American genes, of which the fittest had survived. Lucio, physically, was the refinement of most of the best Italian characteristics. And what he lacked in height was compensated for by the two-inch heels of his boots, so that his and Tess's eyes were level as they stood facing each other.

"Thank you ... grazie, Lucio, I enjoyed the tour. It was"—and here she let her gaze drop to the young man's chest and upper arms—"magnifico."

Lucio nodded and smiled as she turned to go back into the castle. The way women behaved around him had ceased to surprise him, but always gave him pleasure. There was no guile in Lucio. Though he enjoyed female attention, he had to put forth very little effort to attract it. His personal aims and interests were quite simple. When he was ready, he had always thought, he would find a local girl like his mother, marry, and in time, fill the chairs around his own dining table with as many children as his father had.

As a child Lucio had worked in the vineyards, hearing the stories of the Este and Gonzaga families, never trying to sort out the facts from the folklore. In his teens he had worked at the loading dock, taking pride in being able to lift more barrels of wine onto the backs of the trucks than anyone else. When other young men drifted away to the larger cities for work, Lucio stayed in Ferrara at his job with the Gonzaga winery. Without trying, he established a reputation with his employer for loyalty and hard work.

These qualities in Lucio played a large part in Geoffredo Gonzaga's decision to make him manager of the winery. The other workers respected him—he was one of their own. And beyond that, Lucio was easy to control. He had few ideas of his own, but was always willing to see that any orders he was given were carried out.

Life for Lucio was better than he had ever expected it to be. And this new attention from the beautiful American signorina was, if not surprising, unusually pleasant.

46

Tess turned at the doorway of the castle, waved to him and shouted "Ciao!"

Lucio barely heard her voice over the sound of a honking automobile horn, but he knew she was still standing there watching him. So it was hardly surprising that he used only one hand to open the heavy wrought-iron gate for a taxi delivering Andrea Perkins back to the castle.

Six

Andrea paid the taxi driver and started toward the rear of the castle.

"Allow me, Signorina Perkins." Lucio closed the gate behind the departing taxi and took Andrea's suitcase.

"Thank you, Lucio." Andrea spoke to him in Italian. "Since when have you been elected bellhop?"

"Bellhop, tour director, whatever is needed." Lucio grinned. "Everyone is busy today getting ready for the reception this evening."

"Yes, I can imagine." A frigid wind gusted around the side of the castle swirling random snowflakes. Andrea shivered and hunched her shoulders. "If you'll just leave my bag in the vestibule, someone will take it up for me later. I have some work to do in the studio."

Lucio gave her a friendly nod and ran toward the entrance. Andrea turned to go in the other direction. Cold as she was, she paused a moment to glance up at the fresco she had agreed to restore. It covered most of the outside wall of the second floor. In front of it was a narrow walkway flanked by a marble balustrade. The fresco had been painted by an unknown artist and depicted Lucrezia Borgia's entrance to Ferrara.

In Andrea's opinion, the castle itself was an architectural abomination. It would never appear on a postcard. Unlike the Este castle in Ferrara, there were no turrets or moats with drawbridges. Here, they were not needed for protection. The Gonzaga castle sat on top of a hill with the entire countryside visible around it. Thus, the castle sprawled instead of soared.

No doubt there was originally a cohesiveness of design, but succeeding generations had changed the structure to suit their own needs. The third-floor apartment where Geoffredo lived, for example, had been added as late as nineteen twenty. It sat like an oversized railroad car atop the corner of the two wings that stretched out beneath it in a V-shape. The twentieth-century contractor had made a halfhearted attempt to integrate the design with the original. He had added a balcony with a Giotto-type tower patterned after the campanile of the cathedral in Florence. And he had commissioned an artist to paint the ceiling fresco of Jupiter and Juno in the bedroom. But the two lovers looked more like an Art Deco rendering of Mary Pickford and Douglas Fairbanks than native Olympians. However, the major appeal of the third-floor apartment was the modern plumbing and heating, and the magnificent view of the vineyards. It was possible to ignore an eyesore in the interest of comfort, Andrea supposed. What she could not understand was the deliberate destruction of part of the fresco.

Originally, the painter had applied plaster to a solid portion of the outside wall sixteen feet high by forty feet long. Then, covering the entire surface, he painted a tableau of the Duchess of Ferrara's entrance to the city and the retinue of more than a dozen of the exquisitely dressed attendants who accompanied her. But on some fairly recent date, probably when the third floor was added, huge double windows had been cut through the wall whacking off the bodies of a quartet of trumpeters from the trunk up. All that was left were the bells of the trumpets above the window and the musicians' stockinged legs and pointed shoes below. Fortunately, the builder had not destroyed the likeness of Lucrezia or Alfonso, her bridegroom. The harm that had befallen them was at the hands of time and the weather.

The artist had pictured Lucrezia in a dress of gold cloth with purple satin stripes and wide, flowing sleeves lined with ermine. Andrea had finished restoring all of that. She had spent one whole day mixing the plaster from lime, sand, and water to fill in the cracks. While the wall was still wet, she had applied gouache colors that would dry to the original shades the artist had used.

The shadowy members of the entourage that remained, and the figure of Alfonso d'Este, were also finished. Alfonso looked handsome but formidable astride a reddish-brown horse that was draped in purple velvet and golden chains. All that was left to be done was the face of Lucrezia.

Andrea had purposely left it until last. Of course, she would be true to the rendering of the original artist. He supposedly had seen Lucrezia and had recorded the wedding pageant from memory. But on first seeing it, Andrea was surprised at the expression he had given the bride from Rome. It was not what she had expected. For centuries, the name alone, Lucrezia Borgia, implied the embodiment of evil. But the face the artist had painted in the fresco on the side of the Gonzaga castle was not the face of a murderess or a grasping woman without morals. Her features were delicate, and there was a hint of vulnerability about the mouth and eyes.

51

The contradiction between the legend and the face in the fresco was what had set Andrea about her own research into Lucrezia's history, and what had taken her today to the Este castle to see the copy of Pinturicchio's portrait of Lucrezia as Saint Catherine.

Naturally, Pinturicchio had been commissioned to do the painting, and artists seldom put warts on the faces of paying customers. But the portrait and the fresco had been painted in different cities, by different artists, at different times. It seemed more than coincidence to Andrea that both artists, who had actually seen Lucrezia, had found the same sweetness and vulnerability in her face.

From where Andrea stood now in front of the castle, she was looking almost straight up, too close to distinguish the figures in the fresco clearly, but they seemed to be looking back at her.

Above the Giotto tower, dark clouds boiled and diffused and formed again on top of each other, moving quickly toward her in front of the fierce wind. The movement in the sky gave the illusion that the castle was moving, too. For a sickening moment, Andrea had the feeling that the walls were going to fall and crush her.

Seven

The man paused in the doorway of the dining room just for a moment before he began to walk unhurriedly through to make his private search for the girl from Temporary Domestic Service.

It was still early afternoon, but the table was already set for dinner. Ormolu chairs with burgundy-velvet cushions were evenly spaced, five on each side and one at the head. To augment the overcast daylight from the window, electric cut-glass scones were turned on. Their downward glow illuminated delicate Flemish tapestries of floral designs, chosen by a former Gonzaga countess to distract from the "animal aspect" of eating. A gold-leaf frieze next to the ceiling glowed in reflected light and the pink marble floor gleamed from the weekly scrubbing and polishing it had received for several hundred years.

The chef was inspecting the table setting, stopping to hold up each crystal glass and inspect it for water spots. Two maids from the regular staff followed behind him like young quail, watching the chef's face, waiting for his approval.

"Buon giorno," the man said.

"Ah, buon giorno, signore!" The chef's smile bore a hint of surprise at seeing the man there, but he quickly turned his attention back to the table.

The man did not slow or hasten his pace. He passed through the dining room and the kitchen; the girl was in neither room. Checking to make sure he was not watched, the man unlocked and opened the door to the wine cellar and started down the stairs.

Being with her had been a mistake. He seldom took women he barely knew to bed. It was not his style. But the little temporary had been so aggressive and agreeable. He might even have arranged to see her again if she had not started her prattle about the Este family.

"You should be here as *my* guest," she had said.

"Why is that?" He had yawned when he spoke and was giving most of his attention to looking for his shirt, which had fallen behind the couch.

"Because my mother's family has the truest bloodline to the last Duke of Este."

He had held up the starched white apron she had draped over the back of a chair and grinned at the girl. "And this is your inheritance?" It had been an unkind remark, but he could not resist. He was tired of hearing about all the people in Ferrara who claimed kinship with the original owners of the castle. "Was your mother's name Este?" He felt sure it was not.

"Our connection was with the Borgia side," she said. "But we didn't inherit the name."

"You mean the birth of your blue-blooded ancestor was not recorded in the family Bible?"

The girl's face tightened defensively. "Lucrezia Borgia did not have a legitimate birth, either, but no one has ever denied that she was the rightful Duchess of Este."

While the man finished dressing the girl sat in her satin

half-slip and rummaged in her straw purse until she found a bottle of nail polish. She repaired a chipped thumbnail and blew on it until it was dry.

The man was anxious for her to leave. She knew that, but she did not hurry. As she put the maid's uniform back on, she told him the stories she had heard from her mother. The girl was probably embellishing them for his benefit, but still . . .

Before she left, she seemed almost pathetic as she told him of the vow her mother had made her swear, the vow that she would one day try legally to reclaim the castle.

Now, in the wine cellar, the man walked the length of each aisle between the neatly stacked and labeled bottles, looking for the girl. She was not there.

He retraced his steps up the stairs, through the kitchen, then out the rear service door used by the household staff. For all her independent attitude, the temporary girl would never enter the castle by any other door, the man was sure of that. Therefore, she must be somewhere nearby. When he saw the two spots of red on the snow at the foot of the back stairs, he did not realize at first that he had found her.

One red object was hard and sharp; an uneven piece of broken glass that stuck in the vinyl tap on his heel. He paused to scrape it off on a loose stone and saw the second splotch of red on the side of the path.

It was liquid. A spot of something that had dripped on a small mound of snow, leaving a scarlet splotch.

Curious, the man bent down to look more closely. It was spilled wine, he decided. The path to the servants' quarters ran across the top of a ridge. The cypress, scrub, and wild vine–covered earth fell sharply away from the castle on the far side. The first thing the man saw on the down slope was the stem of a broken glass. A few feet beyond lay what appeared to be a shiny medallion. It was, in fact, the decorative overlay from the wineglass. It pictured the red Borgia bull in a golden field of wheat. It had fallen cleanly away when the glass hit a rock and shattered.

Several more fragments of broken glass marked an uneven path to where the foot of the goblet was still held tightly in fingertips that protruded from beneath a stand of low-growing cypress. The nails on the fingers were well-shaped and glistened with polish two shades lighter than the spilled drops of wine that had stained the snow.

The man lost his balance and went down on one knee. To brace himself, he shifted his weight and jammed his left hand down on the ground. A sliver of glass stuck like a needle in his palm and made him cry out with a sound that had the same tonality as the wind.

He did not go closer. The disturbance of the earth where the girl had fallen and rolled beneath the trees was covered—and had been for hours—with a thin layer of snow.

The man got to his feet. He pulled the fragment of glass from his hand and sucked the drop of blood that appeared in its place. Then he hurried back toward the castle.

Someone else would have to find her. Someone else would have to announce that she was dead.

Eight

The chef had finished inspecting the crystal and was giving a silver serving dish an unneeded polishing when the man came back through the dining room. This time the two merely nodded to each other.

Outside the castle, Andrea stood in the driveway for some time after the taxi that had brought her had started back toward Ferrara. She hugged her arms close to her body for warmth as she studied the unfinished fresco. She had turned toward the rear entrance to the castle when Geoffredo Gonzaga called to her from the top of the broad front stairs.

"Ah, Andrea! How nice that you are here again. Could you spare a moment?"

"Of course." She answered with more enthusiasm than she felt. She had hoped to get into her makeshift studio in an unused room near the kitchen before anyone knew she had returned.

Her mind and body still felt somehow disconnected, as though their component parts were not compatible. In the Este Hotel she had wanted to take hold of Aldo Balzani's arm and ask him to stay. But her mind would not strike the spark for action that would let her hand reach out or her mouth form the words.

Later, after he was gone and she was wandering alone through the corridors of the Castle of Ferrara, her body seemed to be taking instructions from some outside source. The prickling at the back of her neck when she entered Lucrezia Borgia's apartment did not stem from her own experience. Nor did the fluttering heartbeat when the door accidentally closed behind her. Panic seemed to hang in the draperies and rise from the floor. It had penetrated her skin and seeped next to her bones like an icy mist.

"It is such pleasure for me that you have returned." Geoffredo smiled and motioned for her to come in, holding the door open.

The stillness of the vestibule was a relief from the incessant whining of the wind, but the Gonzaga castle was only slightly warmer inside than out.

"Did you enjoy Milan?" Geoffredo looked splendid in a chocolate-colored jacket with a hound's-tooth pattern.

"Yes. Very much." His appearance made Andrea conscious of her own dishevelment. Not that Geoffredo looked anything but delighted to see her again, but she felt disapproval from other quarters. Three pompous-looking statues in niches in the wall of the vestibule seemed to be staring at her tattered tennis shoes. In an attempt to pat herself down, she pushed her wind-blown hair out of her eyes with one hand while, with the other, she reached under her rumpled raincoat to tuck the straying tail of her plaid shirt inside the waistband of her jeans.

"The opera season must have begun early this year." Geoffredo looked slightly puzzled.

"The production of *Rigoletto* I saw wasn't in La Scala, it was in a rehearsal hall." Andrea felt a small twisting pain in her chest when she thought of Aldo Balzani standing on the stage looking so pleased with himself in that ridiculous courtier's costume.

"But now you are back." Geoffredo beamed at her and took her arm, guiding her toward the salon. "My home has been desolate while you were gone."

That hardly seemed possible with a houseful of guests, Andrea thought. But she was becoming used to the effusiveness and gallantry of Italian men, especially when they tried to converse with her in English. Her Italian had been passable when she first came to Italy two years earlier; now she considered it quite good. But Geoffredo had insisted on speaking only English, and Andrea suspected that his translations were usually more formal or colorful than he intended.

"And did you go looking again for our Duchess Lucrezia in the Castle of Ferrara?"

"I stopped there this morning to see the copy of the Pinturicchio portrait. I think I can finish the fresco now."

"But you must not finish too quickly." Geoffredo frowned in mock seriousness. "If you finish, you will leave. I must think like Scheherazade and find new reasons to keep you here." He took her hand and kissed it.

Geoffredo's fervor sometimes embarrassed Andrea. As soon as she could without seeming rude, she gently pulled her fingers out of his grasp and said, "It's very nice to see you again, Geoffredo." She took a step back. "There is still work to be done on some of the minor *tarocchi* this afternoon." This was meant to serve as an exit line and also an explanation for her paint-splattered jeans and rumpled appearance.

"But first I must show you something. Perhaps *you* can explain it to me." Geoffredo's eyebrows and hands flew up in bewilderment. He opened a door to the side of the vestibule and stepped back so Andrea could precede him.

The sumptuousness of the salon was in sharp contrast to the austerity of the vestibule. The room was octagonal, with yellow brocade wall coverings and a white ceiling accented with rococo garlands of flowers in pastel-tinted plaster. The walls were covered with gold-leaf framed mirrors and paintings that had been hung there by past Gonzagas who had lived in the castle. The works of the artists who were represented spanned five hundred years but seemed comfortable in each other's company.

"This," Geoffredo motioned to the only painting representative of the last half of the twentieth century. "This is what I wanted you to see." It hung on the wall opposite a carved marble fireplace and was a newly completed painting by Geoffredo's brother Carlo.

The upper half of the large square canvas was alternating horizontal stripes of pure primary yellow and true green, and scattered at random were dollops of black acrylic paint that squiggled and plopped and splattered across the surface. The bottom half of the painting was pure white with a single black dot the size of a dime.

"He calls it, *Afterimage*," Geoffredo said in obvious bewilderment. "Is it good?"

"Ummm." Andrea studied the painting from six feet away, taking in the entire canvas. Then, through narrowed eyes, she concentrated first on the colorful upper portion, then on the stark simplicity of the lower half with its single black dot.

"I insulted my brother by asking him what it meant." Geoffredo clasped his hands behind his back and frowned. "Does it have some special meaning to people who live in America?" He continued to stare at the painting as though he half-expected an explanation to be trailed across the bottom of the canvas in neon letters the way advertisements moved across the buildings in New York.

"No," Andrea laughed, "I don't think it has anything to do with nationality."

"Carlo said he never explains his work, but that this was a testament to everlasting life—as though that cleared up the whole subject."

"Your brother doesn't make small artistic statements, does he?"

"I suppose if you don't understand it either, it's his same old obsession . . ."

Without taking her eyes away from the painting Andrea asked, "What obsession?"

"I think he fancies himself as a—what would be the word—a mystic. Even when we were children, from time to time he would look at me with those cat eyes and say *seriamente* . . . with seriousness . . ." Geoffredo's voice became an ominous whisper, " 'Geoffredo, you and I were born at the wrong time.' "

"What did he mean?"

"That's all he would ever say. I don't know. That we should have lived in some previous age, I suppose. I thought he had forgotten all that foolishness until he brought that astrologer here with him." Geoffredo shrugged. "As to the painting, all Carlo would say was that it illustrates the unbroken links between the past, the present, and the future."

Suddenly, Andrea laughed appreciatively. "Yes! Yes, I see what he means! It's really quite ingenious."

"It's lost on me."

"Stand here." Andrea stepped aside and motioned for Geoffredo to stand where she had been. "Now. Look at the top half, the green and yellow stripes with the black splotches."

"I *have* looked at it from every angle."

"Try it again. And don't look at anything else for . . .

61

until you've counted to thirty. One . . . two . . . three . . ."

Geoffredo glanced at Andrea. She nodded that she was serious. He shrugged and looked back at *Afterimage*.

"Block out everything else from your vision."

Geoffredo narrowed his eyes and counted aloud.

"Let the top part of the painting record itself in your memory."

". . . nineteen, twenty, twenty-one . . ."

"When you get to thirty, shift your vision to the black dot on the white canvas below."

". . . twenty-seven, twenty-eight . . ."

"Don't look at anything in between," Andrea said quickly.

"Thirty."

Geoffredo was silent. Andrea watched him expectantly. "What do you see?"

"Nothing," he said.

"You don't see it?"

"I see a black dot."

"What else?"

"Nothing." He shrugged and turned to face Andrea.

Andrea sighed. "Try it again," she said. "I should have told you what to look for."

Geoffredo stiffened. Ordinarily he would have refused on the ground that the exercise was ridiculous. But for Andrea, he again studied the top half of the painting and began silently counting to himself.

"This time, just tell me when you reach thirty. The magic isn't in the number . . . you just have to give yourself enough time for the image to impress itself on the retina. It's nothing supernatural. It's an optical trick, actually. Something that happens to us all the time, but usually, we just ignore it."

"Twenty-eight," Geoffredo said.

"Now, keep looking at the upper half until I tell you to look at the dot. Don't look yet! But when you do, you should see an 'afterimage' of the green and yellow stripes and the black squiggles. What you're looking at now should appear on the bare white canvas."

"Thirty."

"Not yet! The black dot is just a place to focus your line of vision. Okay. Now. Look at the dot."

Geoffredo frowned in concentration.

"What do you see now?"

"Yes. I see."

"What?"

"I can still see the top half of the picture even though I'm not looking at it anymore."

"The pattern is the same, isn't it?"

"Yes."

"What color are the green stripes now?"

"They're red."

"And the image you see of the yellow stripes . . ."

"They look blue."

"You see, what happens, is,"—Andrea laughed, delighted at sharing Carlo's concept— "you still 'see' the image on the blank background, but your eye transposes the actual color to something roughly complementary. Blue or green becomes red, yellow becomes blue, and black becomes white. Is that what you see?"

"Yes." Geoffredo dismissed the painting with a derisive sniff and a straightening of shoulders as though he had been the brunt of a rather infantile prank. "Clever, perhaps," he said, turning his back on his brother's painting, "but it isn't what I'd call art. The viewer has to do all the work."

"That's the fun of it," Andrea said. "And to some extent, it's really true of all art. Beyond the obvious mechanical part of painting—the technical skill—it's the artist's ability to call up some response, something drawn from the viewer's own experience, that determines whether you appreciate it or not."

"At least it seems my brother and I have one thing in common."

"Oh?"

"My attitude toward his painting is the same as his attitude toward beautiful women. They are to be enjoyed once, and then forgotten." Geoffredo looked pleased with himself, apparently convinced that he could paint a phrase with the same deftness that his brother used in painting a picture.

Andrea laughed.

Encouraged by her response, Geoffredo directed her attention to a delicate Venetian canal scene that hung next to Carlo's painting. "Now this," he said, "is pretty. It is said to have been a favorite of our Duchess Lucrezia, and I can understand why. It looks like what it is."

It was an almost monochromatic scene of a gondola in the Grand Canal of Venice by moonlight. The moon was all but hidden by fog that drifted in front of it in wisps, then thickened and lay motionless around a single boat.

The technique of the painter was above average, not that of a master. But it reminded Andrea of her own first experience of Venice.

She remembered the canal, and the way the outline of Saint Mark's Cathedral and the Campanile had blurred and seemed to float in rhythm with the lazy motion of the gondola in which she was the only passenger. Nearby, an unseen accordion had played "Torna A Surriento," and the sweet sadness of the melody surrounded her, amplified in the mist. Her own gondolier had taken up the song in a clear but slightly nasal tenor. Andrea had turned to look at him. His face was not distinct in the muted moonlight, but she had been fascinated by the swaying movement of his striped shirt as he sang and propelled their boat easily through the fog. When the gondolier reached and sustained the high note of the chorus, he stood absolutely still. The red ribbon that fell from the brim of his flat straw hat hung motionless, then began to quiver as his voice slid away in an appropriate sob as he begged his love to return to Sorrento.

In front of her hotel, Andrea had sat on one of the wooden pilings of the dock and watched the gondolier lower the long narrow pole in the shallow water and push against the bottom of the canal until the sleek black craft slipped back into the fog. The song started again, then faded and abruptly stopped. That night was the first time Andrea had felt that something inside her had detached itself and roamed independently. A part of her had traveled and drifted unseen like the music in the mist.

Today, in the Este castle, in the room where Lucrezia Borgia had lived, Andrea had felt the same division of mind and body, the same detachment.

"Andrea, *carissima* . . ." Geoffredo stood at her elbow.

"Yes. I'm sorry." She forced her attention back to the salon of the Gonzaga castle and the present.

"Do you like the canal scene?" Geoffredo assumed that admiration for the painting was what had so absorbed her.

"Actually, no. There's not enough color. I think I like it less than anything else in the room." The picture had stirred in her the same feeling she experienced in the castle in Ferrara. It was a lack of control, as though her thoughts were being directed by some source outside herself.

She turned and walked quickly toward the vestibule. "I'll be in the studio." Then realizing how rude her abruptness must seem, she turned and said, "I'm looking

65

forward to meeting your brother and his friends this evening." And thinking of her agreement to describe for Geoffredo's guests the background and restoration of the Bonifacio Bembo miniatures, Andrea added, "I'll try to be a credit to you." She gave him her warmest smile and hurried out of the room.

Geoffredo was often a beat behind a conversation with Andrea because of the constant need to translate into English. But a smile; a smile, he thought, was the same in any language. Indeed she would be a credit to anyone, and most certainly to the head of the house of Gonzaga.

Nine

As soon as Andrea had made her hurried exit from the salon, Geoffredo, feeling happier and more confident than he had in some time, opened the wall safe and took out a velvet-lined tray to examine the contents. There would be something there, he was sure, that was appropriate for such a happy occasion.

At that same time, a red and tan Ferrari Mondail Cabriolet left the Via Cavour in Florence and turned north on the autostrada toward Ferrara. The three occupants were en route to the reception for Carlo Gonzaga. Only two of them had been invited.

The two expected guests were Vittorio Sassetti and his wife, Rosa. Sassetti was the curator of the Galleria dell' Accademia that housed the famed Michelangelo statuary and a collection of priceless Renaissance paintings. The invitation to the Gonzaga castle had been hand-delivered to the Sassettis' home. The uninvited guest—and driver of the Ferrari—was Rosa's cousin Caterina Scalona. Caterina had not even had a telephone call. She had heard about the festivities from Rosa strictly by chance. Her first reaction had been surprise.

A week had not gone by for many years when Caterina had not visited Geoffredo Gonzaga in Ferrara or met him in their secret apartment in Florence on the Via Leoni near the Uffizi gallery.

Though Geoffredo had not exactly said so, somehow he had planted the idea that he would be out of town on business for an indefinite time. He would call Caterina when he returned, he had told her.

"A reception? For people from New York?" Caterina's usual composure had briefly fallen away with Rosa's casual mention of the invitation at lunch the previous week.

Rosa knew her cousin well and was baffled by Caterina's unguarded look of astonishment. Rosa, as a result, was embarrassed. And as she always did when she said something she wished she had not, Rosa nervously continued to talk. "The invitation said it was to be only a small reception for Carlo and his American guests . . . and that Carlo's newest painting would be on display in the salon. We accepted, of course, though abstract expressionism is of very little interest to Vittorio." The way she spoke her husband's name, the word rolled and trilled on a three-note scale. "Vittorio's life has been devoted to the Italian Renaissance for so long that nothing painted in the last three hundred years catches his eye," Rosa hurried on. "But I suppose we were really invited because of Andrea Perkins. She has been doing some work at the castle for Geoffredo." Too late, Rosa realized that mentioning to Caterina the fact that a woman had been spending time with Geoffredo— albeit as a hired expert in art restoration—had been a mistake.

"Andrea?" Caterina's dark eyes narrowed almost imperceptibly and demanded more information.

"You probably don't remember her. She worked at the

68

Galleria for a while on a fellowship from Harvard University." Rosa still had Caterina's full attention, and felt compelled to go on. "We were the first Italians Andrea met when she came here. She stayed with us at our apartment until she found a place of her own. Both Vittorio and I are so fond of her . . . almost like parents." *Dio!* Now she had told Caterina how young Andrea was. "Not like *parents*, of course. It's more like . . . Well! You should hear Vittorio when he speaks of her! It's *bella* Andrea this, *cara mia* that . . ." Rosa gave up. She took a deep breath and met her cousin's gaze. "I assumed that you would be at the reception, too. As Geoffredo's hostess."

"You mean *this* weekend!" Caterina's composure, never far out of reach, was again buttoned around her as tailored and trendy as her Gianni Versace suit. "Of course! I'm getting terrible about remembering dates. We'll all go together—you and Vittorio and I. I'll drive."

"We thought the train . . ."

"Nonsense." And Caterina had named the exact time she would arrive at the Sassettis' apartment to collect them.

Rosa knew that Vittorio would object. He did not approve of Caterina—a married woman—and her liaison with Geoffredo Gonzaga. For more than fifteen years Caterina had been the wife of Mario Scalona, who was well placed in the Ferrari division of the Fiat empire. He was also the heir to a considerable family fortune in steel.

Mario Scalona knew of Caterina's affair. But he spent most of his time at the automotive headquarters in Turin; far enough away from Florence so that he was not constantly reminded that his wife was an adulteress. Besides, he believed in marriage. He knew it was important in the eyes of God—his father—and the Fiat Corporation. And so

69

that his marital unhappiness did not become too acute, he had taken an apartment in the automotive city and persuaded his Swiss secretary to accept the spare key.

The fact that Mario was not concerned about Caterina and Geoffredo as long as the lovers kept up some pretense of mere friendship did not change Vittorio's opinion of the relationship. But Rosa knew that if she insisted, Vittorio would agree to share a ride to Ferrara with Caterina just to please his wife. And after Rosa's obvious gaffe at mentioning the reception that she now realized was a complete surprise to Caterina, she felt too embarrassed to refuse her cousin.

Caterina locked in the speed on the red and tan Ferrari as they entered the fast lane. A Mercedes four car lengths ahead of them maintained a comparable speed and comfortable distance. They had been on the autostrada only five minutes when Caterina turned to Rosa, who sat beside her in the front seat, and said, "She's the one with the red hair that always looks like it needs combing, isn't she?"

"Who?" Rosa had anticipated that Caterina would quickly get to the subject of Andrea and was determined, this time, to say as little as possible.

"The girl at Geoffredo's castle."

"She does have red hair."

Caterina asked about Andrea's age; if she was married or had a special gentleman friend; if she planned to remain in Italy; and the condition of her skin. "Working with all those chemicals must take its toll," she said hopefully. Caterina had recently undergone dermabrasion and her face was as fresh and smooth as a child's.

"How long has she been with Geoffredo at the castle?"

Rosa professed that she did not know the answer to any of her cousin's questions. The cords in Caterina's neck were beginning to stand out and Rosa's hands were begin-

ning to clasp and unclasp in her lap. She wished her husband would come to her rescue. But sitting alone in the
back seat, Vittorio was not listening to the conversation.

As always when they were together, Vittorio made
mental comparisons between the two cousins. He had
courted each of them before he married Rosa. When they
were teenagers, the two girls had looked a great deal alike.
Both had slim bodies, smooth olive skin, and luxuriant
black hair that they braided and wore coiled on the tops of
their heads. Rosa's hairstyle had not changed, though the
luster had been dimmed by strands of gray. Caterina's hair
was now layered in a flatteringly short cut, and its original
dark shade was maintained by the most renowned hair
stylist in Florence.

Rosa's figure had rounded and softened. Caterina was
slimmer than she had ever been, and her prominent cheek
and collarbones showed to good advantage in the clothes
designed for her by the House of Giovannetti.

A subcutaneous layer of fat kept Rosa's face firm; skillful
plastic surgery had done the same for Caterina. Both
women had entered their forties, Rosa with mere content-
ment, Caterina with confidence that she could control the
future.

For apparently no reason, Vittorio leaned forward and
patted his wife's shoulder affectionately. Rosa was neither
surprised nor curious. She knew that he sometimes compared the two cousins. And she knew as well as her husband did that he had made the right choice.

"You've met Carlo." Rosa turned toward Caterina, trying to introduce a safe subject of conversation. "What sort
of person is he?"

"He's handsome, in a wiry sort of way . . . and a little
crazy."

"Crazy?"

71

"I don't mean literally, but he's always been different. Geoffredo says his brother has gotten deeply involved with astrology and the occult. Carlo wrote him letters about 'past lives' and his path to the future. Of course, it may just be an affectation. Who can tell about someone who lives in New York?"

"Vittorio." Rosa twisted in the seat and leaned against the car window so that she could look at him. "What did you think of Carlo when he was a student at the Accademia?"

"I didn't." Vittorio preferred not to be drawn in.

"No, truly. Did he seem strange? Did he have talent?" Rosa was genuinely interested in his response, as is any wife who thinks of a question to ask her husband, the answer to which she does not already know.

"Talent? Yes, he had talent. But he squandered it."

"In what way?"

"He was always more interested in the commercial aspects of art than the aesthetic."

"Did he seem a bit strange to you?"

"No more than any other art student."

Rosa smiled. "Did you ever hear him mention having a past life?"

"Certainly not."

"I wonder if he does believe in reincarnation?"

"How would I know that?" Vittorio leaned his head back against the spongy softness of the antelope leather upholstery and closed his eyes, thereby ending his contribution to the discussion of Carlo Gonzaga. He did, however, continue to think of him briefly. Carlo was odd, perhaps, or eccentric might be the better word. But Vittorio had always thought of him as merely overly dramatic; or even lazy. Carlo often left class early, his instructors said, and sometimes did not participate even

72

when he was there. He would not so much as enroll in a class devoted to copying the works of the masters.

Vittorio had heard an amusing story about him over a fine bottle of Vini dei Castelli Romani brought back from a visit to Rome by one of the Accademia's professors. Carlo, the professor said, refused to take the Master's Copy class on the grounds that it was impossible for him to create the works of Ghirlandaio, Filippino Lippi, or any of the other masters scheduled to be studied. The reason Carlo had given (the professor had laughed and attended to the contents of his wineglass before continuing) was that he had not lived their lives. "How can I paint *The Birth of Venus*, for instance," Carlo was reported to have said in all seriousness, "when I've never *been* Botticelli?"

The young fool. Vittorio had remembered the professor's story and laughed about it to himself a number of times afterwards. That was why he was surprised to see Carlo in the school archives one day totally absorbed in studying the color slides of a famous master artist: the miniaturist, Bonifacio Bembo.

Sometime before completing his second year at the Galleria, Carlo left Italy. His absence was noted but not mourned. He had gone to New York, it was said. Later, there were the stories of his fame as an abstract expressionist and his financial success. He had achieved what Vittorio had always believed was his aim.

Vittorio was getting hungry. At least dinner at the Gonzaga castle was something to look forward to. Geoffredo Gonzaga had one of the finest private chefs in northern Italy. Dinner would be superb. Ah, and the wine. That, too, would be a rare treat. Undoubtedly Geoffredo Gonzaga would serve the famous Sangiovese from his private reserve.

It would be good to see Andrea again, too. No one, not

73

even Vittorio himself, had a greater knowledge or deeper reverence for the masters of the Renaissance. He still found it difficult to believe that someone from the United States and trained in American schools could have developed such skill.

Vittorio yawned, but could not doze off. He worried just a little about Andrea. He hoped Caterina would not make an embarrassing scene. And though he did not think Carlo Gonzaga was crazy—far from it, was Vittorio's guess— still, if he chose to make an ass of himself he could be a problem.

The autostrada to Ferrara stretched straight before them. The cruise control of the Ferrari kept the engine at an even, almost imperceptible hum. Soon, Vittorio was lulled to sleep by the monotony.

The subject of Carlo had been abandoned by Rosa and Caterina. Selected mutual relatives were discussed, as was the disappointing schedule of television programs and the difficulty of finding anyone who was willing to do domestic cleaning. As they drove further north, they commented on the surprising snow flurries that melted against the windshield. It was much too late in the year for snow. The two women fell silent for several miles.

Caterina was the first to speak again. "What is her last name?"

"Perkins," Rosa answered without thought or hesitation, then could have bitten her tongue.

Ten

When Andrea left Geoffredo in the salon she crossed the vestibule and entered a wide corridor. The corridor led to a narrow passageway, which opened onto a dark back hall that gave access to the wine cellar, an outside exit, the kitchen, and a number of rooms—some empty, some still used by the household staff to perform the day-to-day chores that insured the smooth running of the castle.

She stopped first in the kitchen to collect the pan of linen rags she had asked the chef to boil for her.

When she agreed to take on the restoration of the *tarocchi* it had seemed practical also to accept Geoffredo's invitation to stay at the castle until her work was completed. There were ample empty bedrooms, he had assured her, and several servants to run errands or lend an extra pair of hands when she needed them. She was also free to choose from any number of vacant rooms to use as a studio. She chose an abandoned hand-laundry room.

It was ideal for Andrea's purposes. There were large windows in two adjoining walls that allowed the maximum amount of northern sunlight to flood all but the far corners of the room. There were three electrical outlets, one midway up the wall next to a fold-down ironing board that she could use for pressing and drying paper and melting wax if she needed it for sizing.

There were two deep basins with hot and cold water. The floor was concrete and had a drain in the center. One wall had shelves where she could store brushes, tubes of paint, packets of pigment, and an assortment of necessary chemicals. She set up a folding aluminum table to use as a work surface, and once her gooseneck lamp was clamped to the table's edge and her box of hand tools and utensils was stored underneath, she was ready to begin.

The tarot cards were in remarkably good condition. They had been preserved in the original "gold-beater's skin" (the outer coat of the intestines of an ox) which had made an airtight seal at the edges. Next, they were placed in a fourteenth-century casket box of dark brown calfskin decorated in a relief design of intertwining vines. And lastly, at some point, they had been locked inside a metal wall safe.

A few of the cards had been attacked by mildew, and some of them were warped and faded. The damage had probably occurred while they were still in use. But, all in all, there was not as much to be done as Andrea had feared.

Some of the paper backing had to be replaced, and to insure that the new paper was as near the quality of the original as possible, Andrea decided to manufacture her own. The first step had been to request the chef to collect and boil a quantity of white linen rags.

That afternoon when Andrea went to collect them, the chef and his staff were still busy putting the finishing touches to the dining room for Geoffredo's dinner party.

Not wanting to interrupt, Andrea looked around the kitchen until she spotted a large aluminum pan usually reserved for cooking pasta on the back of the stove. She peered inside and saw the limp and disintegrating rags floating in several gallons of water that had turned a milky color as it boiled. The fire was turned off and the pan was almost cool, but it was heavy and unwieldy. The water sloshed near the rim as she walked, but Andrea managed to carry it from the kitchen to her studio and set it down just inside the door.

She poured off half of the water into the drain in the floor. Then she began to carefully spread the rags out on the clean surface of a wooden cutting board that she kept with her supplies. She had been absorbed in what she was doing for several minutes when she smelled the smoke.

At first she thought it was coming from the kitchen. But then she realized it was not the smell of burning food. It was wood smoke mingled with the fumes of alcohol or gasoline.

She quickly ran to the hallway. Blazing against the arched stone wall were two wooden crates, the kind used for transporting grapes from the vineyard to the winery. Their flimsy slats snapped and crackled as the fire bit into them. Flames leaped and curled, sending up a layer of black smoke to boil against the high ceiling.

There was no one else around.

Ordinarily, the hall was heavily used. It opened on to the kitchen and Andrea's studio. It also led down into the wine cellar, outside through a service door, and, on the far side, to the back stairway to the second floor.

Instinctively, Andrea ran back into the studio to find something to douse the flames. She quickly returned carrying a sack of sand she had brought to use in repairing the fresco.

"*O, Cristo!*" The chef appeared in the doorway to the kitchen, flailing his arms in panic. Andrea glanced at him and saw that he would be of no help. She began to pour sand in the center of the crates where the flames were fiercest.

"*Aiuta! Aiuta!*" The chef's voice was squeaky and choked with fright, not nearly loud enough to summon help. But Andrea's action spurred his own, and he disappeared through the open door of her studio. In a moment he returned with the pasta pan still half full of water.

"No!" Andrea tried to wave him back with one hand. "No water!"

The smoke was even denser than before, but the flames were beginning to subside.

The chef charged toward the crates with the pan of water, either not understanding or ignoring Andrea.

"*No, non usare l'acqua!*" She flung her arm backward, hitting the chef in the mid-section, knocking him off balance, almost causing him to fall.

The fire was gone now, but not the smoke. Andrea and the chef coughed and stared at each other through reddened eyes.

She apologized and explained that water might have spread the flames. It was wood that they had seen burning, but she was certain that she had smelled gasoline. The chef nodded curtly but did not answer. Then with as much dignity as he could muster he put the pan back in Andrea's studio and disappeared into the kitchen.

Suddenly Andrea felt limp. She managed to open the outside door to help clear away the smoke. The cold, fresh air revived her enough that she was able to make a quick survey of the damage. It was minimal. One part of the hallway's stone wall was blackened with soot, and the floor was littered with chunks of charcoal and a few unburned pieces of wood from the crates. Water had spilled from the

78

pan and made the floor slippery. Smoke still circled the ceiling, but no real harm seemed to have been done.

She began to clear up the mess, picking up the unburned pieces of wood first and looking for a place to discard them.

"No, no, signorina!" The chef was at her side again. He assured her that he would see that the debris was cleared away and the wall scrubbed.

She nodded and went back into her studio. Her knees felt weak. She went to the basin to wash the soot from her hands and noticed they were shaking. As she stood a moment braced against the sink she heard complaining female voices in the hall. They were part of the kitchen staff, she supposed, sent by the chef to clean up.

As they worked, the women asked each other the same questions that Andrea was beginning to ask herself. Where did the crates come from? Who brought them into the hall? Why? Had someone tried to burn down the castle? If that was the plan, why start a fire here; you can't burn a stone wall? Why not in the dining room, or in the salon, or in some room with drapes or furniture that would catch fire?

Whenever there was a pause in the chatter from the hallway, one or another of the women would say ominously, "Signora Lucrezia."

The name had been repeated several times before Andrea understood what was meant. Probably for centuries, she smiled to herself, anything that happened in the castle that could not be explained logically was blamed on the notorious original owner, Lucrezia Borgia.

When the women were gone, Andrea glanced under the stairway and saw something the clean-up crew had missed.

She recognized it immediately. She had brought it to

79

the castle herself as a cleaning agent for the tarot cards. But once she had seen the delicate miniature paintings, she decided not to risk using anything so harsh.

She picked up the can of benzine. There was no question it had come from her own stock of art supplies. DANGER was written across the red can in big black letters in her own handwriting.

Eleven

Andrea put the can of benzine back on the high shelf in her studio where it had been stored before the fire.

She could not imagine who had taken it, or when. Geoffredo had to be told. She was searching on the worktable for her keys to lock the studio when he rushed through the door looking stricken.

"Andrea! I came through the kitchen and heard about the fire! You were not hurt?"

"No. There was no real damage done to anything." She pointed to the shelf. "Someone used that can of benzine to start it."

Geoffredo took her hand in both of his and kissed her fingers. "That someone would do such a thing to you. And the chef said you put it out by yourself."

Geoffredo's concern was comforting, but somehow she felt like a child with a skinned knee being told how brave she was. "I don't think there was ever any danger."

Andrea drew back her hand and smoothed down her hair. Why was it, she wondered, that she felt so clumsy and disheveled around Geoffredo? She supposed it was because he always looked as though he had come straight from a photo session for a color brochure advertising the Gonzaga winery. He was still dressed as he had been earlier, in the dark brown wool jacket, and, though his face was slightly flushed with concern and the exertion of hurrying to inspect the damage of the fire, the starched collar of his shirt showed no hint of wilting and the knot in his tie was still dead center.

"To start a fire in front of your door!"

"It was closer to the wine cellar." But as she said it, she realized that that was not true. It was just as close to her studio as to the top of the cellar stairs. Had the fire been set as some sort of statement—or warning? But what reason would there be for someone to try to frighten her? None, she decided. It all seemed absurd. "The maids who cleaned up the debris seemed to think Lucrezia Borgia had something to do with it."

Geoffredo laughed, but without his usual heartiness. "Ah! Signora Lucrezia. The Gonzagas and Lucrezia get blamed for everything that goes wrong in Ferrara, including the weather." As if in afterthought, he added, "Yes, the fire was near the wine cellar. The culprit must have been someone from the winery." To Andrea it suddenly seemed that he was too eager to accept that explanation.

". . . some unhappy employee," he continued. "In any business there are always a few."

But that had not been his first impression. Andrea said, "Did you think someone was trying to frighten me?"

"No, no! Why would anyone want anything but your total happiness?" Geoffredo dismissed the fire with a wave of his hands and changed the subject. "You were still working?" He glanced at the cutting board with the linen scraps. "I will help you. Tell me how."

Andrea smiled at his willingness. Almost daily since she had been at the castle, Geoffredo had stopped by to offer his assistance, which Andrea gently refused; most of her work could not be done by a novice. But she still was a bit unnerved from the fire and not eager to be alone. "If the chef has a wooden mallet you can borrow, I'll put you to work."

"I shall leave you unattended for five minutes only."

It was less than that when he returned, mallet in hand, and in different clothes. He looked completely out of character in green coveralls of the sort worn by the *cellerari* in the winery. His sleeves were rolled up, and, in his hurry to change, he had even mussed his hair. But it was the shoes that made Andrea laugh out loud. With his garb as a workman, Geoffredo was wearing Salvatore Ferragamo dress shoes.

Though he had no idea why she was laughing, Geoffredo gave her the delighted grin of someone who has succeeded in amusing a child by doing something ridiculous. Andrea liked him better than she ever had before.

She explained the archaic procedure of making paper to him and set him to work helping her. She took her own wooden mallet from the canvas bag beneath the table, and between them, they pounded the fabric to a pulp. For the next step, Andrea took a roll of fine wire mesh from the same seemingly bottomless bag of equipment, and a twelve-inch metal embroidery hoop. The hoop was a remnant from her Girl Scout days and an unsuccessful try at stitchery in an arts and crafts class.

The mesh was cut slightly larger than the hoop. Andrea smoothed it taut across the metal circle and secured it. Next, she returned the pulpy fabric to the pot and diluted it with water until it was a creamy consistency. When the hoop with the mesh was dipped into it, then lifted out again, the water drained away and a sheet of finely felted fibers was left.

Andrea flipped the hoop over like a pancake on the cutting board, then carefully lifted the wire mesh away from the pulverized linen. The wet fibers clung to each other and remained on the board. So that they would dry flat, she placed a clipboard on top of them and weighted it with two bricks.

Geoffredo watched her, fascinated. Then she handed him a hair dryer with instructions to keep the hot air moving around the edges of the pulp until she rescued him from the task a few minutes later.

Conversation between them was much more informal than it had ever been. Geoffredo confided that at first he had been uncomfortable with the inherited title of "Count Gonzaga" after his father's death and that he had no real interest in the business end of running a winery. He was grateful, he said, to have Lucio Trotti for his manager.

Geoffredo was extremely proud, however, of the quality of the wine the Gonzagas had always produced. His finest moment as head of the winery, he said, had come the previous year at a special blind tasting for the world press conducted in conjunction with Banco D'Assagio at Torgiano. Producers were invited to present only one wine apiece, none fewer than ten years old. Geoffredo's twenty-year-old Sangiovese di Romagna won the platinum medal as Best of Show, garnering an incredible average score of ninety-seven on a scale of one hundred.

"Forgive me," he said to Andrea and took a folded piece of newsprint from a Florentine leather card case he fished from the pocket of his shirt. "If you will permit me to read this to you?"

"Of course." Andrea was surprised at the eagerness in his voice.

"This was written by the publisher of *The Wine Investor*, who served as chairman of the international panel."

Geoffredo cleared his throat and read, "The Gonzaga Sangiovese belongs in the Parthenon, a wine against which to measure any ever made. Fruit flavors are astonishingly fresh, the depth of character is awesome, and the balance is impeccable. To have tasted it is to have known perfection."

"I can't imagine any higher praise than that." Andrea smiled.

Geoffredo seemed suddenly embarrassed by his display of pride, and became the realistic businessman again. "The weather that year, and my father's skill in seeing that the grapes were picked at exactly the right time, combined to make such a fine wine. Unfortunately, the quantity was limited. All that was available to be sold, has been. The few cases that remain were never meant for sale. From the beginning they were stored as the private reserve of the castle and served only for very special occasions. You will taste it tonight."

"I look forward to it," Andrea said, this time not looking up from the worktable and the warped tarot card she was repairing. With a small, scalpel-like instrument, she separated the top layer of paper that bore the miniature painting from the moisture-damaged backing. The card was the three of hearts, and on it Bonifacio Bembo had pictured a plump and charming child lulled to sleep in the woods by the music of a flute played by a faun.

Sensing the delicacy of the operation, Geoffredo silently watched her. They both held their breath until the last corner of the miniature came away undamaged from the rest of the card. Andrea sighed audibly; then, in an attempt to continue the conversation about the winery, she said, "You do enjoy your work, though, don't you, Geoffredo?"

"As you do. But perhaps we think too much about business, you and I." His voice had softened, and he let the words fall at random and arrange themselves as they chose, which turned out to be in the form of a question.

Andrea glanced at him with a vague wariness, then quickly looked back at the miniature. "There's a tube of glue on the shelf above the basin. Would you hand it to me, please?"

Geoffredo obeyed. "When you have finished that card, there is something I would like to show you."

"What?"

"Something I brought from the safe in the salon." He stood next to her watching as she spread a thin, even layer of glue on a sheet of paper like the one they had manufactured from the linen pulp. "You know that the castle was built for Lucrezia, the bride of Alfonso d'Este . . ."

"Yes." Carefully Andrea attached the newly restored tarot card to the original filigree ivory backing and trimmed the excess paper with a razor-sharp hand tool. Each *taroccho* was ten times the thickness of a modern playing card, and the ivory backing allowed for almost no flexibility. Andrea had often wondered how the players ever managed to deal them.

"Some of the pieces of furniture and glassware were brought here by Lucrezia," Geoffredo said. "There are other family treasures that were acquired later and preserved by former Gonzagas. Some jewelry. Though we are not sure of the dates, the workmanship would indicate . . ." Geoffredo crossed behind her chair until Andrea could no longer see his face without turning. ". . . that some, a few pieces, date from a very early period."

He stopped behind her. He was so close that she could smell the musky spice of his shaving lotion that traveled with the whispered sound of his breathing.

86

Andrea felt a fleeting, almost imperceptible change in the weight of her shoulder-length hair and knew that he had cupped a strand of it in his palm, then let it fall again. His hands dropped lightly to her shoulders for just the time it took him to say, "*Carissima*, you are a wondrous young lady."

Surprised, Andrea put the restored three of hearts on the table and turned to look up at Geoffredo. The change in mood was too sudden, the timbre of his voice too disturbing. She could think of nothing to say.

"Look out the window at those fields," Geoffredo said, taking her hand and pulling her gently to her feet. He pointed toward the straight rows of staked grapevines that climbed and conquered a ridge and continued up the far hill and down the other side. "That is why I have never married again," he said of the vineyard. "Until now, the winery has been my bride."

The winery might be his bride, Andrea thought, but Caterina Scalona was his mistress. Rosa Sassetti had told her before Andrea ever came to Ferrara. And there had been confirming evidence. Caterina had been in the castle the first weekend Andrea arrived. Though Andrea had not seen her, she had heard Geoffredo in conversation with a woman.

It was late that first night. Andrea was arranging her equipment in the studio when she heard voices in the kitchen next door. The words were not distinguishable, but the female voice was by turn adoring, cajoling, amused, exasperated, and furious. At one point, something heavy had struck the wall, causing the shelves on the laundry-room side to vibrate.

Well, Geoffredo's relationship with Caterina was no concern of hers, Andrea thought. Making her voice sound impersonal she said, "I can understand your feeling for the vineyard . . . especially when you've grown up in a family business it must be more than just a profession . . ."

"That is not what I meant," Geoffredo said. "Here is what I wanted to show you." He took a small drawstring bag made of black velvet from the deep side pocket of the coveralls. "This ring has no recorded history . . ." After emptying the contents into his hand he tossed the bag toward the table where it lit then fell to the floor. Between his thumb and index finger Geoffredo held an exquisite ring in a gold setting. It had a delicate raised mounting of an overlapping leaf design that held twelve or more garnets the size of small holly berries, but the stones were a deeper red. They were attached to each other by delicate, twisted golden stems like a tiny cluster of grapes.

"Ahhh . . ." Andrea reached out involuntarily as she leaned closer to inspect the incredible craftsmanship of the setting and the perfection of the stones.

"It has been worn by some of the past countesses of Gonzaga, but not for more than a hundred years, I think. It should be worn again by someone whose own beauty could never be overshadowed by mere jewelry." He dropped the ring into Andrea's open hand.

Later, Andrea realized she knew what he was saying even then. But at the moment, her attention was totally focused on the ring. "It's extraordinary." She moved it in the palm of her hand, letting the light touch and fire the garnets from different angles. "I've never seen anything to compare with it." She looked at Geoffredo and found that his face was only inches from her own.

"My beauteous Andrea." He took her face in both his hands and looked into her startled eyes. "Since first I saw you it has been like . . ." For once, his careful English failed him. *"Un colpo di fulmine."* A bolt of lightning.

He gently tilted her chin with one hand and kissed her—softly at first—on the lips. His other arm circled her waist and pulled her to him, pressing her hands that held the ring against his chest.

Surprise pinged inside Andrea—first that Geoffredo was kissing her at all, then at the growing intensity of his mouth against her. But most surprising of all was that her own arms reached around him, one hand a fist with the ring inside, the other clutching the back of his coveralls.

"Geoffredo!" A voice boomed from the hallway, then a fist banged on the studio door.

Geoffredo released her. Andrea swallowed hard and took a few steps backward.

"Geoffredo!" The door opened and the intruder stepped inside. He made an instant appraisal of the situation. "Sorry," he said, though he obviously was not. If anything, he seemed amused.

Geoffredo's brother Carlo Gonzaga stood framed in the doorway. Carlo was tall and lean with straight black hair that was thick and unruly. His eyebrows and the corners of his eyes and mouth slanted upward in an impish grin. He wore creaseless, almost colorless corduroy pants and an oversized gray sweatshirt, frayed at the neck and cuffs.

"Hello, love." He nodded familiarly to Andrea. "I was wondering when I'd get to see you."

Geoffredo turned to Andrea and closed his hand over hers with the ring in it. "My brother," he whispered in explanation. "You'll meet him later." Then, almost pleading, "Please wait here just a moment." He hurried toward Carlo, taking the younger man's arm and leading him back through the open door into the hallway.

There was a striking contrast between the two brothers, Andrea thought—the passionate courtliness of Geoffredo and the wild, eccentric look of Carlo.

A bolt of lightning, Geoffredo had said just before he kissed her, *un colpo di fulmine*. Oh, my God, she thought, suddenly realizing that the colloquial usage was "love at first sight." Geoffredo had proposed to her!

A proposal of marriage was where he had been leading all the time. From the beginning, his interest in her had seemed less than professional—nosy, even—but she had never guessed. Why else had he come by to see her every day and insisted on helping her even when the work would have gone more quickly if she had done it alone? Why else had he shown her the ring? Why had he mentioned the previous Gonzaga countesses?

Of course she had known he was interested in her. But her usual rule of thumb with Italian men was to accept their extravagant compliments with the knowledge that for practical application the words should be reduced to half-strength. But Geoffredo was serious—he wanted her to marry him!

And what was that display of her own? She had not been exactly fighting for her life when he kissed her, but love had nothing to do with it. Sometimes your nerve endings did not check in with your brain for messages. Sometimes regret or apprehension got dressed up and paraded around like it was carnival time. But if she were ready to marry anyone right now it would be Aldo Balzani, not Geoffredo Gonzaga.

Sooner or later she would have to face Geoffredo, but she wanted time to think of a gentle, gracious way to refuse. Then what about the ring? If she hurried, she could hand it back unobtrusively while Geoffredo was still talking with his brother. The explanation could come later. Andrea decided to try to slip through the door unnoticed. For the first time, she saw that there were three other men in the hallway. She recognized Lucio Trotti from the winery; the other two, she assumed, were friends of Carlo's from New York.

"I knew you wouldn't mind," Carlo was saying.

"No, no. It is quite agreeable." Geoffredo was trying to hide his irritation. "If Signore Eastman would like to tour the Piedmont wineries tomorrow, the limousine is at his disposal."

Murray Eastman looked embarrassed. "I told Carlo we should wait until this evening to discuss this . . ."

Carlo's glanced shifted to Andrea, and a smile of affection and recognition lit his face. "If it were left up to Geoffredo," he said to her, "he'd probably never let me near you." Carlo leaned casually against the doorway. In his hand was the velvet bag that had held the ring. He had picked it up from just inside the doorway where it landed when Geoffredo dropped it. The younger Gonzaga brother twirled the empty bag around his index finger like a sack of marbles. "It's wonderful to see you again. You look marvelous." In the next instant, Carlo leaned forward and kissed Andrea lightly on both cheeks.

The other three men shifted to one side and cleared the doorway to let her pass. But before she could, Carlo had clasped her by the shoulders. "Absolutely marvelous."

He stepped back, holding her at arm's length, and studied her face thoughtfully. Then, as though assessing changes in someone he had not seen for a long time, he said, "But you've cut your hair." Smiling again, he continued, "I think I like it better this length."

Carlo Gonzaga was not a man one would soon forget. His eyes were flecked with specks of yellow and when he concentrated, the irises seemed to narrow vertically, like a cat's. His speech was often punctuated by a restless hand thrust into his hair, pushing it out of his eyes. There was a constant nervous intensity about him.

Once you had met Carlo Gonzaga, he would stand aside from the faceless mass of acquaintances that marched in and out of your memory. He would refuse to be forgotten. That was why Andrea was doubly sure that she had never seen him before in her life.

Twelve

When Andrea was out of sight at the top of the back stairs, Murray Eastman excused himself from the group of men still assembled in the back hallway and followed her up to go to the guest suite he shared with his wife and grand-daughter.

It was almost time to change for the reception and he was worried about Harriet. He hoped she wasn't drinking already. More than once he had made excuses to their host at a party and helped her home before dinner was served.

The sitting room door was open. As soon as Murray entered he could hear Harriet's voice from the bedroom, then that of his granddaughter Tess.

"I don't see why you get so upset about my staying in Carlo's apartment." Tess's voice had not matured as quickly as her body and still had a teenage shrillness. "There's plenty of room, and I like living in New York."

"I wouldn't object if the housekeeper were there all the time, or some other woman." Harriet spoke softly, in a measured tone that Murray knew could escalate quickly to the edge of hysteria.

"My God! What do you think? That we've got some hot incestuous thing going?"

"Tess!"

"Well, Jesus."

"Your language!"

"All right, all right! In honor of the Italians. *Cristo!*"

"That's another thing. I saw you this afternoon with the manager of the winery."

"So?"

"How did you manage to spend two hours with him? You don't speak Italian, and as far as I know he doesn't speak a word of English."

"We managed to understand each other."

Silence. Murray did not need to see his wife to know that she had closed her eyes and sucked in a lungful of air to try to control her temper. Nor did he need to see his granddaughter to know the challenging look in her blue eyes and the tiny smirk at the corner of her mouth.

"What did you talk about?" Harriet's voice was so soft now that Murray could hardly hear her from where he sat in front of the fireplace in the sitting room.

"Everything. Life."

"What, for example."

"What Italian men expect from a woman."

"And what did Lucio say that was?"

"A man and woman are attracted to each other—they make love—they have babies."

"Tess!"

"What's wrong with that? They usually get married before they have babies. Do you think that's worse than the way my mother lived?"

Murray stood up and started toward the bedroom. If Tess couldn't anticipate the upheaval this conversation was bringing on, he certainly could. He intended to stop it before the situation got worse. But before he could intervene, Tess had plunged ahead.

"Do you think my mother's attitude toward marriage made more sense? She married my father to get away from home. She married the second husband—I can hardly remember his name—she married him because she thought he was going to be elected to Congress. And Carlo, she married Carlo because he was a sexy younger man and she started worrying that she was getting old. And if you think those were the only three men . . ." Tess was sniffling now, like a child—like the little girl her grandmother still chose to think she was. "I was in the second grade the first time I came home from school and saw some guy stuffing his shirttail into his pants when I opened the bedroom door."

"Stop it!" Harriet shouted.

Murray reached the bedroom door just as his wife slapped Tess with all the puny strength she could put behind her quivering hand.

Tess glared at her grandmother and ran toward the door.

"Tess." Murray caught her and held her. She was as tall as he was. But the three quick sobs and the tears that splashed against his neck were the same as when she was a child, when she was so small he had to lift her into his lap to comfort her and the tears reached no higher than his shirt pocket. "Tess, baby."

Tess could not stop an anguished little moan of grief for the mother who had never taken time to know her and the grandmother who did not want to.

Murray Eastman clumsily patted his granddaughter's head. In a moment, she pulled back and whispered, "I'm okay." Then she grinned at him and said, "We don't want to bring on one of grandmother's headaches, do we?"

"Murray, I can feel a migraine starting." Harriet massaged her temples and started toward the bedroom the Eastmans shared.

"I'm sorry, Harriet."

Murray and Tess exchanged glances and hinted smiles. How sweet, Murray thought, that this beautiful young woman came to him for comfort. And how sad were the reasons that she needed comforting.

"I'm sorry, too, grandmother," Tess said, and meant it. She gave Harriet a quick peck on the cheek and watched as Murray solicitously put an arm around his wife's shoulders and guided her toward their bedroom.

Thirteen

Andrea made quick work of a shower, and with her wet hair dripping on her shoulders, shivered into her robe. Leaving damp footprints on the dark tile floor, she ran to the comparative warmth of the bedroom. Ugly but efficient gas logs in the fireplace sent forth unwavering blue jets of flame. The logs were the innovation of the same 1920s architect who had designed Geoffredo's anachronistic third-floor apartment.

Andrea's hair reached just below her shoulders. It had never been longer. She tried to remember. No. It had sometimes been shorter, but never longer since she was a child. So what had Carlo Gonzaga meant, "You've cut your hair?" In the first place, she hadn't. Even if she had, he would have no way of knowing. She had never seen Carlo Gonzaga, never met him before this evening.

They both spent time in New York. He lived there and she was often in the city at the invitation of one of the galleries, museums, or auction houses. But she had never met Carlo Gonzaga. She had seen him for the first time, she was positive, fewer than thirty minutes ago.

Andrea leaned forward toward the fire. The rising heat lifted and began to dry her hair, setting it swirling around her head like the feathered cotton of a dandelion in a light breeze.

The episode in the hallway outside her studio was obviously a case of mistaken identity. If not that, Carlo's performance was meant as some obscure joke for the benefit of his brother.

Andrea's own reaction was still a puzzle. Ordinarily, her composure seldom left her. But she had been flustered to begin with when Geoffredo thrust the garnet ring in her hand. Then, after the strange confrontation with Carlo, she had simply fled, trailing the words ". . . change for dinner" behind her.

What *was* she going to do about the ring? She had meant to hand it back to Geoffredo, but instead, had dropped it into the pocket of her shirt before making her awkward exit.

Brushing her tangled hair back from her face she took out the ring and held it in her hand, rolling it over several times, changing the angle to watch the way the garnets glowed with their own fire in the reflected light from the hearth. Suddenly she realized that somehow the ring's symmetry seemed distorted. In the shadows her fingers cast, she could not carefully examine the craftsmanship of the setting, so she lowered her hand toward the light from the gas jets. The three top garnets, she saw now, were attached independent of the others and lay to one side, revealing a tiny gold compartment about the size of an aspirin. When the garnets were set back in place—a part of the gold-wire vine that held them was fashioned into a hinge—the hollow opening was concealed.

With a surprised intake of breath, Andrea slid a thumbnail under the catch then flipped the compartment open again. Did Geoffredo know this about the ring? Did anyone? Stories about Lucrezia, the notorious original owner of the castle, rushed to Andrea's mind: rings with secret compartments for poison, rings with poisonous prongs that protruded above the setting and when scraped across the skin of an enemy caused instant death.

Andrea set the garnet grapes back in place and weighed the ring in her hand considering what to do until she could privately return it to Geoffredo. She decided it would not be wise to leave anything so valuable unguarded in the room. As long as she was responsible for it she would keep it with her. She wrapped it in a handkerchief and had dropped it in her evening bag when she heard quick descending footsteps on the stairway.

Andrea's room was the closest to the stairs that led down to the vestibule and up to the third-floor apartment. In a moment, there was a polite knock at her door and Geoffredo's voice, "*Cara* . . . Forgive me for the . . . the disturbance . . . in your studio. My brother . . ."

"There's no need to apologize, Geoffredo." Andrea clutched her robe together at the neck, though the door between them was closed. "But there are several things we should discuss." She was careful to keep any hint of familiarity from her voice. Candor and kindness, she had decided, were called for in returning the ring and expressing her feelings, or rather lack of them, to Geoffredo.

She heard a door open down the hall.

"Ah, Signore Eastman." Geoffredo's greeting was hearty and cordial.

". . . sorry my wife won't be down," Murray Eastman's muffled voice filtered through Andrea's closed door, ". . . not feeling well . . ."

Geoffredo made appropriate sounds of disappointment, and then, as another door opened, "Ah! La bella signorina Tess!"

Murray Eastman added, "You look pretty sharp, kid."

The three of them went down the hall to the stairway.

As Andrea dressed, other guests passed her door.

She put on what she had come to think of as her uniform for an occasion such as this. Whenever she was asked to make a presentation of a work of art that she had restored—such as the Bonifacio Bembo tarot cards that Geoffredo had promised to show his guests tonight—she chose the same dress. It was black crepe, draped softly at the shoulders and hips. Black, and a single strand of pearls, she reasoned, would not detract from the restoration, where the attention of the audience was meant to be focused.

She brushed and twisted her coppery hair into a loose cone at the nape of her neck, then pulled it on top of her head, securing it with a tortoise-shell comb. No one could tell how long her hair was this way. She needlessly checked to make sure the ring wrapped in the handkerchief was in her small beaded bag, then left the room to join the others.

Geoffredo stood in the open doorway to the vestibule glancing toward the stairs. He looked resplendent in his usual shades of rich brown. The genuine pleasure that lit his face when he saw Andrea confirmed that he had been waiting for her.

"My dear." He closed the door to the salon behind him, shutting out the homogeneous hum of the voices of his guests. "I must say this all in English in respect for you and your country . . ." Andrea stopped on the bottom step. She knew what was coming next, but still she almost giggled. It sounded as though he were going to propose marriage to the entire United States.

"Tonight I had planned to raise my glass three times. First, I must toast my brother and his return to Ferrara, brief though his stay may be . . ."

The last phrase, it seemed to Andrea, was said with more hope than conviction.

"Second, I must honor the restoration of the *tarocchi,* the work of your magnificence."

As Andrea was deciding whether to stall for a more appropriate time and place to tell Geoffredo that she could not consent to be the Countess of Ferrara, a car drove up in front of the castle.

In his ardor, Geoffredo had not heard it. Whether it was an Italian custom, or whether Geoffredo had gotten an impression of what was proper from an old Hollywood movie, Andrea did not know. But he actually dropped to one knee and took her hand in his.

Andrea's face flushed scarlet. Dear God, the scene played in private would have been embarrassing enough, but they were going to be interrupted at any moment by the new arrivals. She opened her mouth to warn Geoffredo, but he must have interpreted her sudden nervousness as consent or overwhelming emotion. The smile he wore was of sheer joy and triumph as the front door of the castle creaked on its ancient hinges and opened behind him admitting the occupants of the Ferrari, and a gust of chilling wind.

Vittorio Sassetti, Andrea's beloved former boss, stood holding the door for his amiable wife, Rosa.

"Vittorio . . . Rosa . . . how wonderful to see you!" Andrea jerked her hand out of a startled Geoffredo's grasp.

Geoffredo got quickly to his feet with as much aplomb

as he could muster. Even someone who was watching closely would have hardly noticed the pause, the slight falter in his step when he turned to greet his invited guests and saw that the Sassettis had not arrived alone.

Framed in the doorway like a mannequin in the window of the Salone Roberta di Camerino on the Via Delle Grazie, stood Caterina Scalona, the reason for Geoffredo's frequent trips to Florence for the past ten years.

Caterina's mink cape was thrown back over one shoulder. Her left arm akimbo, the hand rested gracefully on a stylishly protruding hip bone beneath her bottle-green silk dress. Caterina's chin was tilted upward in a studied pose that allowed her to lower her eyelids just enough so that her straight-on gaze was through thick, dark eyelashes. She seemed completely immobilized, cast in wax or carved from wood, except for the vein that throbbed in her throat.

There was no question that she had taken in the scene the moment she entered the vestibule.

"Caterina . . ." Geoffredo struggled to mask his surprise.

Before he could say more, both Caterina's hands went to his face and held it in front of hers. Then her arms slithered around his waist and well-manicured fingernails dug into the back of Geoffredo's wool jacket. As Andrea and the Sassettis watched, Caterina kissed Geoffredo full and hard on the mouth.

After an embarrassingly long moment, she loosened but did not relinquish her grip. She leaned back and smiled at her lover. "Rosa insisted that I come with them." Her voice had the dark richness of cappuccino.

Rosa Sassetti, with a small sigh, gazed at the skylight above the vestibule. She was accustomed to her cousin's convenient lies, but would never approve of them.

"And I do want to see Carlo again." Caterina brushed Geoffredo's lips with a long slender finger. "You forgot to tell me when he'd be here." She linked her arm in his and gently turned them both toward the salon, never once glancing at Andrea.

Vittorio, who seemed grounded against the electricity that ricocheted around the hallway, hugged Andrea and vigorously kissed both her cheeks. "We have missed you, *cara.*"

Rosa, who was not unaware of the tension but at a loss to think of a way to ease it, said the first thing that came to mind. "I have heard wonderful things about your chef, Geoffredo. The finest in Ferrara, I'm told."

Fourteen

Harriet Eastman opened the door to the sitting room a crack and peeked in to see if it was empty—to make sure that Murray and Tess had gone downstairs to the reception in the salon. Satisfied, she fetched a tumbler from the bathroom, and a bottle of vodka from a shoe bag in her suitcase.

There had been three bottles, but two of them were already empty. She filled the glass two-thirds of the way and was surprised to see that there was no more left in the bottle. She had thought there was more than that.

The room was dark except where she had left the door open to the other room. Sitting on the side of the bed she sipped from the glass and stared at the motes of dust that drifted and danced in the strip of light. She wondered why you could not always see them. They must always be there. That seemed as good a thing to think about as any. She blew her breath in that direction several times and watched the way the disturbance made the tiny particles dip and dive.

After a while she began to hum to herself. "Country Gardens," that was the name of the song. How many thousand times had she heard her daughter practice it on the piano? Harriet laughed silently and shook her head. Such a naughty little girl! How she had hated to practice the piano. Harriet and Murray used to chuckle over the wild excuses she could invent. Once she said she had to rest her fingers, because if she kept stretching them across the keyboard her hands would get bigger than her feet and she would grow up looking like an ape.

Harriet lifted the glass, expecting a generous swallow of vodka, but there were only a few drops left. She checked the bottle she had set down on the floor beside the bed. Surely it was not empty already. It was. Then she examined the other two bottles in the shoe bag, just to be sure. There was nothing in them, either.

She reached for a post at the foot of the bed to steady herself and stood straight, smoothing her dress over her hips with the other hand. Maybe she should go to the reception. She could simply go down to the salon and say that she felt better and had decided to attend the reception after all. She wondered if they were serving cocktails or wine.

As she started toward the door to the sitting room, her thigh hit the edge of the dressing table. "Aww!" Reaching to turn on a floor lamp next to it, she heard a tinkling crash at the same moment the light came on. She could see now that she had knocked over a heart-shaped picture frame she always carried with her. Inside was a black-and-white photo of a little girl wearing an enormous hair ribbon and clutching a terrified-looking kitten.

The glass from the frame was broken, and shards littered the top of the dresser. A few fragments had fallen on the tops of her shoes. One had stuck in her stockings, and a runner crept up the outside of her leg as she watched.

106

Oh, God, why! Why had her daughter grown up? Why had her daughter died?

Harriet wiped at the smudged tears on her face with the back of her hand. She felt almost sober. That was not how she wanted to feel.

Going to the reception would mean changing her stockings now and fixing her makeup. And she would have to face Murray's pity, and Tess's acceptance.

Aimlessly, she walked out into the empty hall and down the back stairs. She had no particular destination in mind but a vague plan to go outside for a few minutes to fill her lungs with fresh air—she was concerned about all those tiny particles of dust she had been breathing.

When she reached the first floor she found herself in a part of the castle where she had never been before. There were several doorways at the bottom of the stairs. Straight in front of her light showed beneath a heavy door, and pleasant cooking odors seeped from around it. The kitchen. If someone asked, she would simply say she had come for a pitcher of water.

Soundlessly, the door swung open when she leaned her shoulder against it. She blinked in the bright light. A man in a white apron, the chef, stood over the sink with his back to her, washing and trimming artichokes. With the sound of the running water he had not heard the door open, nor did he know that she was there. Steam rose from several copper pots on the stove, and plates, ready to be filled, were stacked on a counter next to where she stood in the doorway.

Behind the stacked dishes, in a neat, triangular arrangement, were several bottles of wine waiting to be uncorked. On an impulse, Harriet grabbed one and hurried back into the hallway.

I'm a sneak thief, she told herself. Surely someone knows how many bottles had been there. There was no question that the one she had taken would be missed. But she felt exhilarated, almost lighthearted. Shoplifters must feel like this, she thought. It was exciting to get away with something—to commit a crime and not get caught.

Giggling like an adolescent, she hurried back up the stairs to her bedroom.

The Swiss Army knife she had bought in Geneva had everything from scissors to a toothpick on it; there was bound to be a corkscrew. And there was room in her shoe bag for one more empty bottle.

Fifteen

The light in the salon came from several different sources. Two dozen low-wattage bulbs had long since replaced candles in a chandelier of crystal prisms that cast spectrums of refracted light on the ceiling, the carpet, and the gold-colored fabric that covered the hexagonal walls. A fire flickered in the white marble fireplace and danced shadows around the room.

In front of the wall where Carlo Gonzaga's painting *Afterimage* hung was a sturdy metal easel which held a transparent thermoplastic case containing the *tarocchi*.

Andrea had carefully laid out the sixteenth-century tarot cards on a length of black velvet stretched across a sheet of four-foot-square plexiglass. Another hard transparency the exact size of the base was fitted on top and the two were clamped together holding the delicate Bonifacio Bembo miniatures securely in place.

The response of Geoffredo Gonzaga's guests to the exhibit varied from Carlo's speechless awe to his stepdaughter's glancing lack of interest.

Because of the proximity, it would have been impossible for Carlo to escape the unintentional contrast between the *tarocchi* and his own painting. His *Afterimage* was a well-executed optical trick. The miniatures were inspired genius.

"They're tarot cards!" The surprise in Tess's voice made Carlo laugh.

"*Tarocchi* is the Italian word for tarot." Carlo led her toward a white linen-covered table that had been set up as a makeshift bar against the opposite wall. "Whiskey with ice, and for the signorina, a small sherry," Carlo instructed a tuxedo-clad barman. "What did you think *tarocchi* meant?"

"I don't know. But why all the excitement just because they're old?" Age, except her own, held little interest for Tess.

At eighteen, she wanted to look at least twenty, and had chosen the dress she wore with that in mind. The shoulders were bare, and folds of pale blue jersey falling from a beaded cuff that circled the neck were nipped in at the waist by a narrow silver belt. Either the dress or the open smile attracted Lucio Trotti. The handsome young manager of the winery quickly crossed the room and the two began an exchange of primitive English and fractured Italian heavily accented with sign language.

Carlo was glad to be relieved of the chore of entertaining his stepdaughter. Since neither Tess nor Lucio had anything of interest to say, in Carlo's opinion, the fact that they spoke different languages would probably prove to be an asset. Carlo surveyed the room.

Andrea was near the fireplace with the Sassettis. Geoffredo, with Caterina still close at his side, joined them, then escorted the small group around the room, introducing the American guests to Andrea and the visitors from Florence. Carlo was the last to be approached.

He spoke charmingly in Italian with the Sassettis about their glorious home city and his days as a student at the Accademia. To Andrea, he smiled with disturbing familiarity and, leaning close to her, said in a voice too low for anyone else to hear, "I completed a portrait this afternoon that I'd like you to see. It's totally different from the work I've done the last few years . . . more in the style I used before. You'll remember. It's like other paintings of mine you used to admire so much."

Perplexed, Andrea turned to look more closely at Carlo. No, she was convinced she did not know him. She was about to say that the only painting of his she had ever seen was *Afterimage,* when Geoffredo began his announcement.

"If you would all please be seated," Geoffredo said to the room at large. "Perhaps, gentlemen, if you will move the chairs a little closer to the easel . . . yes, there, that's fine . . . Miss Andrea Perkins will tell you something of the restoration she has just completed."

Geoffredo bowed to Andrea with a proud and affectionate smile, then took a seat at the end of the front row. He skewed his chair toward the exhibit and purposely or not, turned his back to his brother's *Afterimage.*

Sammy Hirschfeld was the first to think of a link between the *tarocchi* and Carlo's painting. He had suggested it one Friday afternoon the previous January when he visited his client's apartment.

That morning in New York had not gone well. Sammy woke to find that the freezing drizzle of the past few days still fell in quiet apathy on the city. He had a head cold and felt miserable even before he opened the Hirschfeld Gallery. Then, a prospective buyer, an ophthalmologist Sammy thought had decided to purchase *Afterimage* for his waiting room, called to say he had chosen a photographic panorama of the skyline from a downtown studio instead.

Deciding to break the news to his client in person, he had walked the four blocks to Carlo's apartment. By the time Sammy reached the lobby and stood waiting for the elevator he was chilled, sneezing, disgruntled, and depressed.

The lost sale was not so bad for Carlo, Sammy thought almost grudgingly. Carlo would survive. He did not have Sammy's expenses. The exorbitant rent on the gallery and the advertising rates in the art and architectural magazines were only two of the many bills that came due each month. But the artist never seemed to be concerned with money. Carlo was the King of Comp. He lived almost rent-free in this elegantly renovated Eighty-sixth Street apartment building because he had painted a mural for the lobby. He drove a Cadillac Seville because he had designed the fabric for the upholstery and posed for a magazine ad. To Sammy's knowledge, Carlo had never paid for a meal in a New York restaurant, or tickets to the theater, concerts, or sporting events.

The elevator door slid open and Sammy stepped in and pushed the button for the top—twenty-fifth—floor. You had to give Carlo credit, Sammy thought. He had learned the secret of being a "personality." His black lion's-mane hair had become almost as famous as Dali's moustache or Picasso's bald head.

The elevator stopped and Sammy crossed the hall and entered the open door without knocking. Carlo's corner apartment had a floor-to-ceiling window with a view of the Hudson River and an adjacent balcony that looked down on Manhattan. The partitions that had divided two small bedrooms from the living and dining areas had been removed so that what remained was one large room the size of a tennis court. At one end was the platform where Carlo spread his huge canvases. Stacked on the floor and on three low shelves were cans of paint and a haphazard grouping of brushes and other paraphernalia the artist used in his work.

Two paint-splattered tarpaulins served as carpets. There was one quite ordinary-looking couch that folded down into a bed, and scattered in front of a brick fireplace were a number of oversized cushions and three transparent inflatable plastic chairs. Back issues and current copies of art magazines were piled in uneven stacks in two corners of the room.

Fletcher Kimball was seated on the floor next to the window. In front of him was a tape recorder that he was listening to intently through earphones.

God, Sammy thought. Dealing with Kimball is all I need to make this day a total disaster. He stepped around the astrologer who looked up and nodded an expressionless greeting as Sammy crossed the room.

Carlo, at a stand-up draftsman's board he used as a desk, had the latest issue of *American Art Quarterly* spread in front of him. "Ah, Sammy! I'm glad you're here. Have you seen this?" He waved the glossy magazine that was folded open at a two-page color spread at his manager.

"What is it?"

"An article on the current exhibit at the J. P. Morgan Library."

Sammy frowned at the periodical. It was just one more injustice. The Morgan Library probably got a flashy feature article without paying a penny for it. "You mean this—the Renaissance miniatures?" He tilted the magazine toward the gray daylight from the window and inspected it more closely.

"Yes. They're on display all this month."

J. P. Morgan, an avid collector, had accumulated a number of Bonifacio Bembo miniatures painted on tarot cards. They were only occasionally put on display and then under the strictest security. The rest of the time they were kept in darkness, locked away from the elements so that the rich, brilliant colors used by the sixteenth-century painter would not fade.

"I hadn't thought of them for years," Carlo said.

"You've seen them?"

"Not the Morgan collection, but similar ones at the Gonzaga castle in Ferrara."

Suddenly Sammy was very interested in the article. He read the captions beneath the color reproductions and whistled softly at the monetary evaluation the writer of the article had assigned to the collection. "Your brother has a set of these?"

"I'm sure it's not a whole set . . ."

"Tell me what you remember about them." Sammy wanted to know everything: the name of the artist, when they were dated, and most importantly, how amenable Geoffredo would be to an American exhibition if the paintings proved to be valuable.

Carlo's answers were vague. He had not seen the miniatures since he was a child, he said. But on one issue he seemed definite. He felt sure that his brother would never agree to anything as ostentatious as a commercial exhibit.

Fletcher Kimball had not been listening to the discussion, intent on what he was hearing through the earphones. Suddenly he jerked them off and ran the audio tape backward, filling the room with the irritating metallic whir.

"Fletcher, turn that damn thing off!" Carlo said.

"Wait! You have to hear this again," Fletcher Kimball

insisted excitedly. "This is the fourth time you've had a titled incarnation. I *thought* I heard you say your name was Lord Rickling last night, and now that I've played this tape several times I'm sure of it."

Kimball turned up the volume and ran the tape forward. The voice was unmistakably Carlo's, but he was speaking with a British accent in a somnolent cadence as though he were hypnotized. Which, Sammy Hirschfeld deduced, his client had been when the tape was made. "Carlo, for God's sake," Sammy said, "what is he talking about?"

Carlo merely thrust a nervous hand through his tangled hair. He turned and looked out the window through the gray afternoon drizzle, across the tops of the neighboring buildings to the river. His attention seemed focused on the sluggish progress of a barge as it inched its way upstream.

Kimball turned off the machine, and the room was filled with welcome silence for a moment. Then the astrologer said, "Carlo is truly an extraordinary subject. I feel fortunate to be his spiritual guide. In his very first psychic session he identified himself as a Hittite prince who was killed by the army of Ramses II." In a voice tinged with awe he said to Carlo, "Do you realize your present life is your fourth incarnation in nobility? There was the Hittite prince, first, then a Bavarian king, this British Lord Rickling you discovered in our session last night . . . and your present title of Count Gonzaga."

"I've told you before, I *have* no title." Carlo looked sternly down at Kimball who was still seated on the floor. "Of what use is a title in America?"

Sammy Hirschfeld, unsuccessfully trying to delay a sneeze, searched his pocket for a handkerchief.

"In America, of course not. But in Italy . . ." Fletcher Kimball persisted.

"And I have no title in Italy, either."

"But your father was a count."

"And my brother—the oldest son—is a count. It's called primogeniture."

"That's not still legal, is it?" Kimball seemed a bit crestfallen.

"No. But then neither are titles." Carlo went back to the drafting table and picked up the *American Art Quarterly* again. "Until Geoffredo has children, I am what is known as the heir apparent."

Fletcher Kimball tried not to show his disappointment. He had counted on using Carlo's title in a brochure he had in mind. He and Carlo had discussed the possibility of inviting a small but select group of "previous being" believers to a "life search" seminar. An ideal location for such a gathering, Kimball had suggested, would be the artist's ancestral castle. Carlo had said he would query his brother on the possibility of using a wing of the castle that was currently unoccupied.

Kimball tried not to press Carlo about it. He knew, at this point, Carlo merely found the idea amusing. Geoffredo Gonzaga, Carlo had said, might agree to such a plan, but only as a favor to his brother, not because he would ever approve of such an unorthodox gathering. Still, without the artist's knowledge, Kimball had mentioned the upcoming "Italian Experience" to four of his wealthiest clients, all of whom were eager to be included. "Heir apparent," Fletcher Kimball said. "That sounds impressive, too."

Carlo laughed. "There is only one thing that is of less importance than being an Italian count in the contemporary world—and that is, being the younger brother of an Italian count in contemporary Italy. I found that out at an early age. That's why I came to New York."

"Carlo, we have some business to discuss." Sammy

Hirschfeld stood and turned his back to the astrologer, hoping to exclude him from the conversation.

"Even bastard sons used to have exalted status." Carlo put a hand on Sammy's shoulder, not yet ready to be pulled back to the present. "If a titled father could give his love child a name, he gave him land and an army or possibly a title and rank in the church. When I was a child I felt truly cheated that I wasn't going to get an army. I used to pretend I was illegitimate, hoping that might change things until my father convinced me there weren't any Gonzaga armies left—not even for Geoffredo." Carlo grinned, then turned a serious face to Sammy. "The painting didn't sell, is that it?"

"At least this buyer decided against it. But there are others . . ."

"No. I think I'll keep this one and hang it over the crack that's developing on the wall next to the kitchen."

"*Afterimage*? Is that the painting you're discussing?" Fletcher Kimball refused to be ignored.

Carlo nodded.

"It's the finest thing you've ever done," Kimball said indignantly. "It's a visualization of the whole of life, isn't that the way you see it, Sammy?"

"It's an excellent example of abstract expressionism," Sammy said for the benefit of the artist, and meaning it. Then to tie the astrologer to reality, he added, "What I see is perfectly mixed colors—yellow and green stripes—on the top half that reverse themselves in the spectrum when the eye adjusts to the lower white background. It's a beautifully executed artistic concept." Sammy immediately switched his attention to the magazine photographs of the Morgan miniatures as though the discussion were ended.

Kimball had more to say. "Those are the words of an art dealer—a businessman. I see the past in the colored stripes, the present in the black dot on the white field, and the future in the eye's remembered image. I see . . ."

"Carlo," Sammy, concentrating on the *American Art Quarterly* to shut out the sound of Kimball's voice, had come up with the first thread of an idea. "Are you serious about not selling *Afterimage*?"

"Yes. I like it."

"Does your brother have any examples of your work?"

Carlo brushed his hair back in his habitual gesture. "No. Somehow I can't see the Gonzaga castle as a proper setting for my painting."

"Perhaps not permanently. But if Geoffredo were to be presented with such a fine example of your talent . . . and later, the suggestion were made that an exhibit of past and present art treasures from the house of Gonzaga would be of great interest here in America . . ." Sammy was counting on the possibility that Geoffredo Gonzaga might see such a tour as beneficial to his untitled younger brother. It was reasonable to think that he would consent to an exhibit that would include the Renaissance miniatures—if they were of comparable quality to those of the Morgan Library—for that reason alone. The Gonzaga family owed Carlo something! Surely Count Gonzaga could see that.

Carlo's laughter shook his lean frame. "Yes! I like the idea," he said. Then, seriously, to Sammy, "I can't imagine Geoffredo allowing the miniatures to leave the castle, and I have no idea of their condition at any rate, but I do like the idea of having one of my paintings hung in the salon. How can he refuse?"

"I'm sure he wouldn't want to . . ." Sammy was not to give up his plan so easily.

"And Murray Eastman can deliver it for me. He's going to Ferrara this spring to negotiate a contract with the Gonzaga winery for exclusive American distribution."

Fletcher Kimball could see a plan forming that did not include him. Grasping at an opening where he could slip in he said, "No, Carlo! You should deliver it yourself. Think of it. To get away from this . . ." he threw out both arms toward the freezing drizzle that obscured and blurred the New York skyline. " 'O Sole Mio', and all that. We could," he deftly slid the plural pronoun in, "talk with him about accommodations for the seminar . . ."

Carlo was not unaware of the motives of the other men. But the crust that had formed over his childhood resentment had begun to crumble lately, and the thought of seeing his homeland again after several years' absence was suddenly appealing.

So a letter suggesting the restoration of the *tarocchi* had been sent. Geoffredo agreed, for his own reason, to legitimize the cards that won the castle and the vineyards for the Gonzaga forebear. Alitalia had been contacted. They supplied first-class tickets for Carlo and his entourage, and the trip was planned.

Gazing at the bleak New York sky and contrasting it with the memory of warm Italian sunshine on his back, and the memory of the smell of newly turned springtime soil in the vineyards had contributed heavily to Carlo's decision.

And now, ironically, here in Ferrara in March, the ground was frozen and snow was falling.

Andrea adjusted the lights attached to the plexiglass case that held the *tarocchi* so that the group in the salon could view the display without glare. She waited a moment longer until everyone was comfortably seated before she began to speak.

"I was originally consulted on this project by Count Geoffredo Gonzaga as a sort of referee," she began. "My job was to be similar to that of a casino boss in Las Vegas who checks the playing cards when there is a disputed game of blackjack."

There was a smattering of laughter.

"Even though the card game in question was played some three hundred years ago between a Gonzaga and an Este forebear, we were looking for some lingering evidence of chicanery. The saying goes, the cards never lie. Isn't that right, Mr. Kimball?"

The astrologer was pleased to be consulted as an expert and returned an affirmative smile.

Andrea continued. "It was with relief that I was able to report to Count Gonzaga that none of the *tarocchi* showed any evidence of illegal markings. I found no dog-eared corners or secret symbols on the backs. And with what we were able to discover, the evidence tilts in favor of the honesty of the Gonzagas. Unfortunately, there can never be conclusive proof. There was always the possibility of a confederate sending signals behind the back of one of the players, or a quick peek at a tilted hand. We weren't even able to verify the entire deck because unfortunately it is not complete, two of the fifty-three cards are missing."

Some of the people in the room realized that the outcome of the ancient card game where the stakes had been paid and the dispute was nothing more than gossip, was of little consequence compared with the value of the Bonifacio Bembo miniatures. If monetary value was to be assigned, the worth of the *tarocchi* far exceeded that of the castle, the grounds and the winery combined. A printed evaluation would read "priceless."

Sammy Hirschfeld leaned forward in the chair behind Carlo. "The Morgan collection can't hold a candle to this one," he whispered with a proprietary grin. Carlo shrugged.

"Instead of evidence of ill-gotten gains," Andrea continued, "I found that each of the cards is a miniature painting in which Bembo depicted the appropriate symbol of the *tarocchi* with exquisite skill and subtlety and wove in clues to the mysterious life of his benefactress, Lucrezia Borgia. All of the four suits: swords, cups, coins, and staves, and the fifth suit of trumps, are represented. Somehow the wild card, the Fool, even survived. And if you've ever watched an Italian card game, you know how extraordinary it is that any one of these cards came out undamaged."

That's the God's truth, Murray Eastman thought. The damned Italians get too emotional about everything. And that included his host, Geoffredo Gonzaga. Months ago, Murray had nailed down an agreement for exclusive distribution of Gonzaga Lambrusco—papers had been signed, dates had been set, American orders had been taken—now Gonzaga says there will be a delay in delivery. All Murray asked was that the Gonzaga winery meet the terms of the contract. You'd have thought he had suggested that Geoffredo realign the planets. Even though Murray was a guest in the castle, he intended to make it clear to Geoffredo the way Eastman Company did business.

"Later, be sure to examine all the *tarocchi* individually," Andrea continued. "Many of them have tiny portraits or landscapes painted into the fabric of a dress or the empty space of a letter. For example, the 'S' in the card, La Stella, The Star, has the face of Lucrezia in the upper part of the letter. And with a magnifying glass you can recognize the doorway of this castle in the bottom curve.

"In the rank of the cards, the Star came immediately after Hell. This, apparently, is due to the influence of Dante. You might remember that at the end of the *Inferno*, Dante and Virgil emerge from the depths of Hell to see the stars in the upper air, and that each of the three books of the Divine Comedy ends with the word 'stella' or star . . ."

Lucio Trotti had no interest in art, and his mind would have wandered even if he could have understood what the American signorina was saying. He did not feel at ease in a dress suit and tie, but that was only the least of the reasons for his discomfort. If he were seated nearer the door, he would be tempted to leave. And not just the castle—he might leave Ferrara. His brother in Rome could find him a job. Running a finger around the inside of his collar he stretched his neck and glanced around the salon. He was impressed with the opulence. No wonder the Estes had thought for centuries of reclaiming the castle.

"Unfortunately, La Luna, the Moon card, is missing. It was almost certainly a portrait of Lucrezia." Andrea pointed to a spot left vacant on the *tarocchi* display. "The Moon triumphed over the Star because she was bigger and brighter . . ."

Andrea would have beautiful children, Geoffredo thought. She would give him daughters with silky red-blond hair that would blow across their faces as they played on the slopes above the vineyards. And boys—sturdy boys with dark eyes and strong limbs who would learn to plant the vines and harvest the grapes. Geoffredo smiled to himself thinking of the announcement of the birth of a Gonzaga heir. The bells in the cathedral would ring. Perhaps the city's artillery would even fire a salute.

"According to Ovid, Luna, the Moon, had a carriage with two wheels that was drawn by two horses, one black and one white." Andrea paused and, almost as an aside, said, "We can only imagine what was on the missing Luna card, but I think Bonifacio Bembo would have pictured Lucrezia as the moon in a golden carriage . . ."

Sammy Hirschfeld pressed his springy red hair down

with one hand wondering if he should take his barber's advice not to part it so close to his left ear. So what if the bald spot showed? At least his hair would lie flat.

Sammy sighed and let his eyes and thoughts circle the salon of the Gonzaga castle. How come Geoffredo got all this and Carlo got nothing? Carlo said it was the Italian oldest son syndrome. Geoffredo had gotten the vineyard, the winery, the castle, and even the title of Count. And what about the *tarocchi*? Whom did they belong to—only Geoffredo? Carlo could probably contest possession of them. What were the laws? As Carlo's business manager, Sammy had spoken to him about consulting lawyers on both sides of the Atlantic. Surely an Italian will could be broken. But litigation could take years. A more immediate solution was called for. Whoever owned those Bonifacio Bembo miniatures would be set for several lifetimes.

And that was another thing.

Sammy was sick of all that reincarnation crap Carlo and Fletcher Kimball were always talking about. Carlo had always seemed too cynical to fall for anything that idiot had to say. The astrologer had been invited to Ferrara to view the tarot cards that had told the fortune of Lucrezia Borgia, Carlo said. But the way he kept snooping around the castle you'd think he was planning to buy it.

Forget that bastard, Sammy told himself. Keep things in perspective. Carlo needed to be reminded of the possibilities open to anyone who owned the *tarocchi*. Sammy mentally began to arrange the Hirschfeld Gallery for the first American exhibition. He could imagine the favorable comparisons the press would make between his collection and that of the J. P. Morgan Library.

"You might be interested in some of the materials Bembo had to work with in painting the *tarocchi*." Andrea turned toward a small table beside her and indicated an exhibit she had arranged for Geoffredo's guests. "The paintings were executed on vellum, a fine parchment made from the skin of sheep, goat, calf, or pig. This happens to be calf, because it is the most supple and has the finest grain. The paint is watercolor, made from gum acacia and pigment. To get the thin but opaque effect, the artist would first dampen the vellum, then he floated the color on in washes. If he made a mistake, and I suppose even Bonifacio Bembo made a few, he most likely used the same substance I did to clean the surface: newly baked bread, though I hope his temptation to eat the eraser wasn't as great as mine. Count Gonzaga's chef brought still-warm, fresh-baked loaves every day for me to use for this purpose."

Cute. Very cute. She's a cute girl, that Andrea Perkins, Fletcher Kimball thought. Though he did not understand why Carlo was so keen to have him, Fletcher, work up her astrological chart. Of course it was impossible without her cooperation, and there had not been an opportunity to talk with her privately, yet. Fletcher would guess, though, that she was a water sign.

Fletcher Kimball was not a charlatan. He truly believed in astrology. He had given up a job with a faltering advertising agency to study the occult. But he also believed that interpretation of signs was left to the skill of the practitioner.

He saw his own future successfully linked with Carlo, the Gonzaga castle, and the Renaissance tarot cards. Kimball still clung to the idea of the seminar, but once he arrived in Ferrara, he had a revelation that also involved the Gonzaga winery. God. What a magazine layout it would make. A picture of Carlo—identified as one of the foremost abstract expressionists—standing in front of *Afterimage.* And Fletcher Kimball—identified as one of the

124

foremost exponents of the abstract—holding up one of the Bonifacio Bembo tarot cards. On a table there would be a bottle of Gonzaga wine, and the copy could read something like, "From the good fortune of the Renaissance to the good taste of today."

You could tie in the Eastman Wine Distribution Company and maybe one of the more prestigious New York galleries—maybe even Hirschfeld's, if Sammy changed his attitude and was willing to give Fletcher the respect he deserved.

Fletcher Kimball was certain that the future could be read in the stars, and it could also be shaped by anyone who was clever enough to do it.

"The gold overlay that accents the brilliant colors used by the artist," Andrea said, "is exactly what it appears to be, pure gold. For this, Bembo would have made arrangements with someone from the society of gold-beaters, one of the local guilds, to hammer coins into layers thin enough to be cut and shaped and glued to the vellum.

"Gilding has been done since very early times. The Romans used thick sheets, or leaves, of gold. The word 'thick' is relative, of course. But by the time of the Renaissance, gold-leaf was beaten to a thickness of about one two-hundred-thousandth of an inch."

Caterina Scalona had managed to claim the chair next to Geoffredo's. Rosa Sassetti was invited to sit there, but Caterina unobtrusively managed to persuade both Rosa and Vittorio to move down and leave the chosen spot next to the host for her.

Legs crossed, a silky slender knee touching Geoffredo's thigh with just enough pressure to remind him constantly that she was there, Caterina wore a look of serenity. Her expression implied that she was giving full attention to Andrea's presentation. She *was* thinking of Andrea. Her

thoughts were, *"Lei deve sofrire e morire in gravidanza."*
May she suffer and die in childbirth.

Caterina knew that Geoffredo's major disappointment in life was that he had no children. There was no young Count Gonzaga to inherit the name, the history, or the fortune. That, to Caterina, accounted for her lover's attraction to the young American art restorer.

Geoffredo and Caterina had become lovers when they were both disillusioned by their marriages—marriages smiled on by the church. If the nuptials had not actually been arranged, at least they were lovingly sanctioned by their respective families. Once Geoffredo and Caterina met, his wife had never been a problem for Caterina. By the third year of being Countess Gonzaga, the bride, who had been rather plain to begin with, fell victim to complacency. Her hips broadened, her complexion dulled, and a note of stridency crept into her voice. She had known what was expected of her and managed to get pregnant twice in the first three years. Both infants were stillborn. And in the depression that followed, Geoffredo's wife had not had the heart to survive the malaria brought on that particularly wet spring by the vicious mosquitoes swarming up from the Taro River that flowed near the castle.

But this one—this Andrea—could not be so easily dismissed. She was young. Caterina did not linger on this thought. Age was the one area she could not control. Andrea was beautiful with a fresh, natural vibrancy. Caterina was also beautiful, but she depended more and more on her hairdresser, her masseuse, and settings where the light was flattering.

During their first two years, Geoffredo might have consented to divorce and remarriage. But even then Caterina had known, and had foolishly confided to Geoffredo, that she could not have children. And now she was past forty, childless, and trapped in a boring marriage.

She studied Andrea, the center of everyone's attention. A bit narrow in the hips, Caterina thought. Perhaps she could not bear children, either. The thought was pleasing. But if she could, Caterina wished it to be twins. She deserved to become pregnant with twins and suffer twice. Big, fat, rosy boys that would crack her pelvis like chicken bones, then fade and die like their mother when they reached the air. Caterina smiled at the thought and let her hand rest possessively on Geoffredo's shoulder.

"The origin of tarot cards has been the subject of a great deal of speculation." Andrea knew this was sticky territory as far as Fletcher Kimball was concerned, but it was data she had uncovered in her research and pertinent to the history of the cards. "They are virtually never used in the Anglo-Saxon world except for fortune-telling. As a result, they are surrounded by a strange mystique and a lot of nebulous theories."

"They originated as religious tablets in the temples of Ancient Egypt," Fletcher Kimball said in a stage whisper to Carlo. "The designs are corruptions from Hebrew or cabalistic signs. It was the gypsies who brought them to Europe from Egypt." His interjection came from the same inspiration that leads someone to sing ahead of the melody to prove he knows the lyrics.

Andrea pretended not to have heard Fletcher Kimball and continued. "Actually, they originated right here in northern Italy . . ."

Kimball smiled knowingly in disagreement.

". . . not far from the Gonzaga castle. The name, tarot, *tarocchi,* was taken from the local tributary to the Po, the Taro River.

127

"The American fascination with tarot fortune-telling came much later than you might suspect. It was taken up from a French friend and popularized by our favorite national scoundrel-genius, Benjamin Franklin."

"My dear, if I might speak . . ." Fletcher Kimball's agitation had raised the pitch of his voice several notes and set his fingers fluttering in the air for attention.

"In a moment, Mr. Kimball. I have just one more thing to add. Though Lucrezia Borgia and her friends may have whiled away hot and sticky summer afternoons playing cards and gambling, she never had her fortune told with the *tarocchi*."

Andrea quickly concluded her presentation and made a small bow to the polite response on the part of some of the guests and the enthusiastic applause from Geoffredo, Carlo, and the Sassettis.

Speaking to small groups was always more nerve-racking than addressing a hall full of people, which Andrea had done on occasion at universities and museums. She reached in her evening bag for a wadded-up tissue to wipe her damp palms. When she looked up, Fletcher Kimball was unfolding his long skinny legs. His thin, sharp face was flushed a deep pink and when he started toward her with a quick shrug of the shoulders, for a moment Andrea had the impression of watching an angry flamingo ruffling its feathers.

Sixteen

Andrea closed the clasp of her handbag and put it back on the display table that held the *tarocchi* box and some of the props she had used for her presentation.

Fletcher Kimball cut an uneven path toward her, dodging the other guests who had stood and begun to move about.

Vittorio was quickly at Geoffredo's side. "Count Gonzaga, with your permission, the Galleria dell' Accademia would be honored to be the first to display such an impressive addition to the wealth of Italian art. It seems only proper that the Bonifacio Bembo miniatures should first be shown in their native country . . ."

"As you know, I've been your brother's business manager and agent for several years . . ." Sammy Hirschfeld, not one to wait for a lull in the conversation, began an extravagant description of his New York gallery overriding Vittorio's entreaty.

Tess quickly cornered Lucio Trotti and headed with him toward the bar.

Caterina remained seated and watched both Geoffredo and Andrea.

Murray Eastman fumbled for his glasses and went to inspect the miniatures again.

By this time, Fletcher Kimball was at Andrea's elbow. "Your work as a restorer is marvelous, Miss Perkins, but I'm afraid your information about the tarot is incorrect," he said in a condescending voice. "They did originate in Egypt, you know ... and the symbols were inspired by Egyptian mystics and astrologers."

"I don't pretend to be an expert in the field of the occult, Mr. Kimball, but I do thoroughly research every project I take on. I'd be happy to show you my documentation ..."

"It's your contention, then, that Lucrezia Borgia did not believe in the supernatural?"

"Yes, yes she did! She had a crystal ball. There was a popular belief in the early fifteen hundreds that if you concentrated and peered into the crystal you could see the future."

"And *I* can document that astrologers were among the most powerful advisors to the aristocracy," Kimball said.

"I don't deny it. But their method for foretelling the future was to open the Bible and read the first phrase that struck their eye. There's the story about a favorite poet of Lucrezia's who, before starting off on a visit to his sick brother, read the scripture 'He fell asleep with his fathers and they buried him in the city of David.' Sure enough, the brother was dead before the poet could get there."

"Still ..."

"They read their future from the Bible, not tarot cards."

"Excuse us, Fletcher." Carlo Gonzaga stepped between them and took Andrea's arm. "I'd like to speak with Miss Perkins privately for a moment, if you don't mind."

Andrea was glad to be rescued and smiled her appreciation. The smile lasted until she realized that Carlo had maneuvered her out of the salon and into the vestibule.

"This will take just a few minutes," Carlo said. "I'd like you to see the portrait I mentioned."

"But I can't leave right now. Geoffredo said dinner was to be served immediately following . . ."

"I'll return you to him soon. Dinner is always later than you expect it to be in Italy. Surely you've discovered that." He still held her arm. Andrea wavered, but saw Fletcher Kimball watching her from the doorway, and let Carlo guide her toward the stairs. "Besides, if we are going to be related—if you are going to be my sister-in-law—we should get better acquainted."

"I don't know what you're talking about." Dear God, the presumption of this man. How did Carlo Gonzaga think he knew so much about her? They were at the top of the stairs. Andrea stopped and started to turn back. "I really must get back . . ."

"Come on." Carlo grinned at her. Letting go of her arm, he walked ahead and opened the second door on the left. Andrea followed.

Carlo's room was a jumble of paints, palettes, and canvases. It smelled of turpentine.

He switched on a desk lamp and aimed it at an easel that stood nearby. "You mentioned the Luna card," he said, "one of the missing ones . . . the one with Lucrezia's portrait."

"Yes." For a moment Andrea thought Carlo must have it, must have known where it was all along. "Did you see it when you were a child?"

"No. But my image was the same as yours. You mentioned the symbol of Luna in her two-wheeled chariot with the black and white horses." Carlo picked a miniature painting up from the easel and held it in the palm of his hand, studying it. "I didn't have any Renaissance gold-beaters to help me with the materials, so I had to resort to acrylic-gold number eighty-three. Otherwise, this seems to be the way you described it."

He balanced the small portrait back on the ledge of the easel and adjusted the light once more. Then he motioned for Andrea to come around to see it.

It was a portrait of a young woman in a chariot holding an upraised whip over the backs of two horses—one black, one white.

Carlo had pictured Luna dressed in a dark-colored gown similar to the one worn by Lucrezia Borgia in the Vatican mural depicting her as Saint Catherine. She wore a red cloak and a brimless sable hat banded with rubies. Her hair was the color of wheat and streamed about her shoulders and to her waist.

It was a skillfully executed painting—indeed, executed with skill to rival that of Bonifacio Bembo himself.

"When I barged in on you and Geoffredo in your studio this afternoon, I had just finished this," Carlo said. "I suppose that's why I was so surprised to see that you had cut your hair."

The serene and confident face in the miniature that looked full into Andrea's eyes was not the face of Lucrezia Borgia. It was Andrea's own.

Seventeen

"Surely you're not surprised that I saw you as Lucrezia." The expression on Carlo's face gave no hint of explanation. He merely seemed amused.

The portrait of the young woman was exquisite in its detail. The figure was no wider than three-quarters of an inch across the shoulders from puffed sleeve to puffed sleeve. The fabric of the dress was black and patterned with royal blue and gold Maltese crosses. Above the squared-off bodice, a gold chain glittered around the slender neck of the young beauty with the compassionate face—Andrea's face.

It was unmistakably Andrea. The wide eyes were the same shade of green. The mouth with the full lower lip was hers. Even the blue veins near the temples were there in the portrait and seemed to be throbbing as Andrea's were now. "You work very fast," was the only reply she could think of. But no matter how fast he worked, how could he possibly have painted her at all? "It hasn't been two hours since the first time we met," she said.

"Since the first time we met *here*. Since the first time we met during this century." Carlo reached across the desk and picked up a slender paintbrush which he brandished like a toy saber. It was a meaningless gesture—like a child balancing on one foot or pulling at the sleeve of his jacket to divert attention when he doesn't know what the reaction to his words will be. It was as though Carlo, with his nonchalance, was saying—it's all quite commonplace, quite ordinary, really.

"Actually, the painting was finished early this afternoon," he said, "long before I walked in on Geoffredo's ardent proposal of marriage to you and our subsequent hasty first meeting here at the . . ." He wrote the words in the air with the tip of the paintbrush and dramatically read them aloud as he wrote, "Castello . . . di . . . Gonzaga . . ."

She obviously was not going to get a sensible answer from Carlo. Whatever his explanation might be, Andrea decided she did not want to hear it. She was behind the desk where Carlo had guided her to get the best possible view of the painting on the easel. She made a move to leave, but Carlo was blocking the way. One more step in his direction and she would have to push her way past. For the moment, she stood still.

"Geoffredo did ask you to marry him, didn't he?"

"I'm not going to discuss it with you. And, I'm going back downstairs." Her statement was meant to dislodge Carlo. It did not.

"I saw the ring."

"He did show me a ring. I suppose it's been in your family for centuries. Naturally, Geoffredo knows how interested I am in all sorts of Renaissance art."

"But he wants you to be his next countess." Carlo grinned at her. "And he wants a . . ." He wrote the words in the air again, "Count . . . Geoffredo . . . di . . . Gonzaga, JUNIOR." He added a vigorous imaginary exclamation point.

Andrea laughed. She could not help it. Count Geoffredo di Gonzaga, Junior, sounded so absurd.

Carlo laughed, too. "I'm not a clairvoyant," he said candidly. "I knew of Geoffredo's intentions toward you because he confided them to me. And may I say that I would be pleased and honored to have you as a member of the family." He gave her a comic bow and hurried on before Andrea could interrupt. "The other fact that you and I have met before in some previous existence—is just as clear to me, and just as certain."

"Carlo . . ." Andrea made again as though to leave, but Carlo ignored her attempt at a graceful exit.

"Reincarnation is difficult to accept right at first. I understand that. The usual way would be to have Fletcher Kimball hypnotize you and lead you through regression by stages. But the argument I would have to give to convince you to let him do that would take time, and frankly, I would find the whole ordeal boring. It's always boring to have to convince someone of something you're sure of, don't you agree?" The question was strictly rhetorical, and no space was provided for an answer. "It all seems so obvious, and I can feel how receptive you truly are, although, understandably, you're not willing to admit it yet. But the spirit you had then"—Carlo indicated the portrait of Andrea as Lucrezia—"has survived. And with it, all Lucrezia's strength and courage."

He was like a man strapping her into a roller coaster. It isn't dangerous . . . no need to be afraid . . .

"How could anyone without an enormous amount of courage have traveled from Rome to Ferrara by horse-drawn carriage to marry a man she had never seen before? You were only twenty years old! There were no close friends traveling with you, no family members, only a paid retinue. No. You're no coward."

135

"And I'm not Shirley MacLaine, either."

Carlo laughed and dropped the paintbrush back on the desk top. "I know I'm going too fast. I tend to do that when I feel passionately about something. But you do feel some kinship with Lucrezia whether you're willing to admit it or not. You've sensed the truth that her enemies were jealous of her beauty and intelligence and made up monstrous stories about her." Carlo paused briefly this time for an answer from Andrea but got none. "If you are strictly a disinterested observer, why did you agree to do the restoration of Lucrezia's tarot cards and the fresco of her wedding procession?"

"I was hired by your brother—who, incidentally, probably wonders where we are this very moment."

"But why take on *this* project? You must have had other offers. I understand your services are very much in demand. There must be many more interesting places to work than Ferrara. Why did you come here?"

Carlo's playful attitude was gone. He turned and looked intently into Andrea's eyes. She was startled by his sudden change of mood. Instinctively she backed away from him. To brace herself she leaned against the desk. Her hand hit the slippery cover of an art magazine, the top one in an untidy stack. They began to slide apart. Two hit the floor, some scattered across the desk top. Andrea picked up one that had landed in a swivel chair next to her and tossed it on top of the others. Then, with equal parts of anger and embarrassment, she said, "Carlo, I don't know what this is all about, but I have no interest in, nor knowledge of reincarnation."

"Just tell me why you chose to come to Ferrara?"

"The project interested me. I was anxious to see the Bonifacio Bembo miniatures . . . and the fresco."

Andrea knew that Carlo's strange eyes were searching

her face for a flicker of agreement, a flash of recognition. She knew this, and stubbornly wanted to deny any interest but a professional one in Lucrezia Borgia. Still, for an instant, the unreasoning fear she had experienced that morning in the Este castle in Ferrara returned. She remembered her near-panic when the door closed behind her in Lucrezia's apartment. She had felt totally abandoned. Everyone she loved, it seemed, had deserted her—left her alone to face a terrifying and unknown future.

There was a slight twitch at the corner of Carlo's mouth as though he were going to smile and say, "I knew . . . I knew all along . . ."

He touched Andrea's shoulder with one finger. "You've felt Lucrezia's spirit ever since you've been here. It hasn't all surfaced in your consciousness yet, but . . ."

"We have to get back downstairs," she said decisively. "We've been gone too long." Andrea reached up to brush his finger away, but Carlo's reflexes were faster than hers and he gently caught her hand and held it.

"You aren't wearing the ring," he said.

"I am not engaged to Geoffredo." Andrea was openly annoyed now and jerked her hand out of his, then lightly pushed at Carlo's chest to get past. She was eager to get back to the salon for another reason. Until Carlo reminded her again, she had forgotten about the garnet ring in her evening bag. She felt sure it was exactly where she had left it. However, she was responsible for the safekeeping of the valuable piece of jewelry until there was an appropriate time when she could return it to Geoffredo.

"Forgive me. I'm blocking your way," Carlo said, as though the thought had not occurred to him before. "Just a moment and I'll move the easel out of your way."

Andrea stood waiting while Carlo first turned the easel, then carefully collapsed the legs and leaned it against the wall. As he did, he said, "There's still so much of the spirit of Lucrezia left in you. I think she must have been your original self. I, on the other hand, am getting close to nirvana." He spoke with something that approximated a chuckle. "I know these terms are off-putting, but I can't think of any other way to say it, except that I'm convinced that my . . . soul . . . has transmigrated. To Americanize it, I'm like a star tailback with the football tucked under his arm about to race over the goal line. Whereas you are still a rookie sitting on the bench. My main problem is that I was born out of sequence this time. When I showed up in the locker room I was issued the wrong uniform, so to speak."

Andrea started for the door. "Carlo, I'm leaving."

"Yes. We should be getting back. They'll wonder what's happened to us," he said as though it were a totally original idea.

Andrea swept past him and started to turn to the right toward the front stairs.

"This way is faster," Carlo said, motioning toward the opposite end of the hall. "And we won't have to make a grand entrance down the sweeping stairway." He took Andrea's arm and led her toward the back stairs. "If it were your former self who was going to marry my brother and if this were still the fifteen hundreds, they'd insist that Geoffredo prove his virility. God knows in Ferrara they may still do it." He laughed. "I wouldn't be surprised if the Town Council insisted on it."

Andrea decided that Carlo's conversation, as well as his painting style, was abstract expressionism.

"The local people have clung to so many of the old traditions, if they insist on reviving that one, you'll have no one to blame but yourself."

"What are you talking about?"

"You're the expert who says there is no way to prove whether our Gonzaga forebear won the castle fair and square in that card game with the Duke of Este."

"What possible difference could that make now. It was three hundred years ago."

"True. But half the people in Ferrara already maintain they are kin to the Estes and still feel they have a claim to the castle. Naturally, they realize it would never stand up in court. But when you and Geoffredo get married . . ."

"Carlo, I don't want to hear any more of your nonsense."

"You can understand their concern," he went on blithely. "This is no reflection on you. It's just local custom. But if there are children from this union—if there is to be another little Count Gonzaga born—they'd want to make sure, at least, that he was the legitimate son of the present Count."

They were at the top of the back stairs. Andrea took hold of the railing.

"Don't take any of this personally." Carlo was one step behind her, talking as fast as he could, and obviously finding his bizarre monologue highly amusing. "What's at stake here is establishing Geoffredo's virility. After all, you know how important it is to the aristocracy to propagate the line. With all the research you've been doing on Lucrezia, you've probably read an account of how something like this used to be handled. In fact, as I remember, when Lucrezia's first husband fell out of political favor with her father, Pope Alexander—how's that for a great line, 'her father, the Pope'?—anyway, when her first husband fell out of favor, the Pope insisted the bridegroom was not a properly functioning husband, and, though the couple had been married for more than a year, and there are no recorded complaints from either party, Lucrezia received a divorce because her husband refused to submit to the test. The test itself was regarded as scientifically accurate. There was no grading on the curve, it was strictly a pass or fail situation. And it was simplicity itself, because there is really only one way for a man to prove to the satisfaction of the Town Council that he isn't impotent, and that is to perform in front of witnesses."

Andrea tried to concentrate on the dimly lit stairway and ignore the chatter of Carlo Gonzaga behind her.

"There are two possibilities of how such a test could be administered under properly dignified circumstances. Ideally, the participants should be the husband and wife. In the case of you and Geoffredo . . . now, we're just talking hypothetically here, but this is the way it would have been done when Lucrezia was the Duchess of Ferrara. Some neutral place would be agreed upon. As far as the present Town Council is concerned, the most convenient location would probably be the Este Hotel."

"I'm not listening."

"Actually, that would be a good choice. The Este is very good about setting up business meeting rooms. I can't see that there would be a need for a P.A. system or a podium, but some extra chairs could be sent up from the ballroom to the bridal suite for the Town Council . . ."

Andrea giggled in spite of herself at the ludicrous picture he had conjured up.

"Of course the bride doesn't have to participate. It can always be some other, disinterested lady. We're merely talking about local custom because I know you're interested in history. You must have heard of this ceremony before. You may even have read about the most famous case in our family. It was in Mantua, sometime in the mid-fourteen hundreds, where Vicenzo Gonzaga, the prince of

140

the reigning house, gave an audience of ambassadors and cardinals proof of his virility upon a *virga intacta*.

"If, as Geoffredo's wife, you choose not to participate, they might require something similar of him, and that could be trouble. I'm not sure there are any virgins of legal age still around. You see, that's one of the areas where modern law conflicts with ancient custom. A girl used to be thought marriageable and bedable at twelve. Now . . ."

They had reached the bottom of the stairs opposite Andrea's studio. The room was dark, but the door was open and from inside came the unmistakable sound of someone being violently sick.

Andrea ran across the hall and flipped the light switch. Doubled over the cold water basin was one of the kitchen maids. She blinked in the light and looked up at Andrea and Carlo, then turned her head and was sick again in the sink.

"What is it? What's the matter?" Andrea hurried to the girl, grabbing a clean cloth from her bag of supplies on the way. She dampened the rag and pressed it to the girl's forehead.

"Grazie." The maid's body was still shaking with nausea.

"Is it something you ate or drank?"

"No, signorina. It's . . . in the kitchen."

Carlo was already at the door to the kitchen and swung it open.

"I can't even stand to be near someone who is sick," the maid said, as Andrea hurried after Carlo. "And when I saw that . . ." She turned back toward the sink.

The kitchen had been modernized only the year before. One of the features most prized by the chef was the dropped ceiling of suspended sheets of opaque plastic that concealed a network of fluorescent tubes. The resultant diffused light replaced shadows with an overall blue-white glow. That was one reason the body lying on the floor looked so ghastly.

The knees had hit the floor first and the angle of the fall had thrown the shoulders backward, leaving the legs doubled under at a grotesque angle. The eyes were open, staring, beginning to bulge. The lips had swollen and parted, exposing clenched teeth.

In the unnatural light, the liquid that was splattered on the side of the cabinet and smeared on the floor looked purple. In daylight, or by candle and in a crystal glass, the wine was a full, rich red. When he fell, the bottle had slipped from the chef's hand but had not broken. The label was old, but unsoiled, and read Sangiovese di Romagna.

Eighteen

The maid, who had been the first to find the body of the chef sprawled on the kitchen floor, haltingly made her way to the servants' lounge. Vagrant snow flurries blew around her on the dark path behind the castle. The chill wind in her face and the need to concentrate on skirting small patches of ice diluted the horror of what she had seen. The lounge was empty when she entered. She stretched out on a couch near the gas heater and pressed the wet cloth Andrea had given her against her forehead. In the darkness behind her closed eyes the image of the chef's face and the thought of the fire earlier that afternoon alternately surfaced and submerged and became the same. "Lucrezia," she said through chattering teeth. Tomorrow, as soon as it was light, the maid promised herself she would leave the castle and never set foot here again.

Andrea watched until the girl had crossed the path and the door to the lounge was safely closed behind her before going to the salon to find Geoffredo. The guests were milling about, some examining the *tarocchi*, some chatting in groups of twos and threes. Rosa and Vittorio Sassetti stood with the young Tess Gonzaga in front of the *tarocchi* dis-

143

play and were attempting to describe to her the Italian significance of the miniatures painted by Bonifacio Bembo. Geoffredo stood near the arched doorway with the ever-present Caterina Scalona at his side. Opposite her was Fletcher Kimball, holding her hand, palm up, as though he were reading it. For once, Caterina was giving someone other than her lover her attention.

From Geoffredo's smile when he saw Andrea come through the vestibule, she knew he had been waiting for her. With a hurried excuse he left Caterina and Fletcher Kimball and came to meet her, his hand reaching for hers.

"Geoffredo," Andrea said when he was near enough that she could speak without anyone else hearing, "in the kitchen . . ." She took his arm, as much for support as to emphasize the urgency. "There's something you have to know about."

While Andrea was gone, Carlo had stood guard in the back hallway to make sure no one else stumbled on their grisly discovery.

In the fluorescent pall of the kitchen, Geoffredo's face blanched, then turned ashen, when he saw the grotesque figure on the floor. He leaned for a moment on the doorjamb for support, then coughed into a folded white handkerchief and cleared his throat. "I must call an ambulance."

"The police, first, I think," Andrea said softly.

A call to the local *stazione di polizia* had seldom gotten such attention. One, perhaps two, officers might have been expected to investigate the report of a death where no violence was indicated. But when the captain discovered who had made the call, he led the way to the police car himself, taking three uniformed men with him.

The daily police blotter usually was filled with reports

of domestic quarrels that needed mediation, and accounts from female tourists of purse-snatching by young thieves on Mopeds. But this, from the first sketchy information, was presumably a poisoning at the Castello di Gonzaga. Not only the police, but everyone in Ferrara would be interested.

As it happened, by the time the captain and his men arrived at the castle, there were two deaths to investigate.

Murray Eastman was more concerned than usual about his wife. Not that Harriet's excuse to be alone tonight was any different from her excuses of many nights before. But the scene with Tess had been upsetting for all three of them. And Harriet's headaches were becoming more frequent lately.

What he saw when he opened the bedroom door had not surprised him. The room was almost dark. Only the lamp next to the dressing table was on. Harriet lay sprawled on the bed, her face to the wall. One shoe had dropped to the floor. Her dress, which she had unbuttoned but not removed, was twisted around her. On the bed table was an empty vodka bottle. Next to it was a Swiss officer's knife, the corkscrew extended. Crumbs of cork were scattered on the tabletop and floor, and one large chunk floated near the top in an almost full bottle of Sangiovese di Romagna.

Murray had removed his wife's remaining shoe and was straightening her dress when he glanced at her face. Even in the dim light he saw its odd contortion. He tried to tell himself it was a trick of the exaggerated shadows that stretched and languished in the room. But he knew that was not true. He knew she was dead before he lifted the unnaturally heavy wrist to feel for a pulse.

Murray ran back toward the salon to summon help,

knowing, but not admitting to himself, that if assistance of any kind were available, it was no longer needed by Harriet.

He reached the foot of the stairway in the vestibule at almost the same instant that Geoffredo Gonzaga was ushering the policeman from Ferrara in the front door. In his state of shock, Murray thought his host had somehow anticipated what he had to say. "She's upstairs," he told the first policeman. Then to Geoffredo, as an explanation, or perhaps an excuse, he said, "She didn't usually drink wine."

It was not long until everyone in the castle knew of the two deaths. Both bodies, it also was known, had been found with open bottles of the prized Sangiovese di Romagna nearby.

One policeman was dispatched to the servants' lounge to question the employees of the castle. Two were sent back to the police car for flashlights with instructions to search the grounds for, as the captain put it vaguely, "anything that might seem suspicious." After a cursory investigation of the kitchen and the Eastmans' bedroom, the captain himself joined Geoffredo and the guests in the salon.

Murray Eastman sat stunned and silent on the couch. His granddaughter Tess was beside him, holding his hand.

Carlo Gonzaga, his face in a rare state of expressionlessness, leaned against the wall next to his painting, *Afterimage*. Fletcher Kimball sat nearby on the floor, cross-legged, and seemed to be trying to put himself into a trance. His eyes were closed, and occasionally he made an almost imperceptible humming sound.

Lucio Trotti perched stiffly on the edge of one of the ormolu chairs looking as though he wished he could trade his tight collar and dress suit for the loose coveralls he wore each day in the winery.

Caterina Scalona sat with her legs crossed at an angle to show the long, smooth curve of her calves. One elbow was propped on the upholstered arm of her chair; her chin rested on the flat of her hand and was upturned to displace the faint wrinkles that sometimes crisscrossed her neck.

Andrea took a space saved for her between Rosa and Vittorio Sassetti on a long couch.

The captain of police, a courteous man of middle age, had never been inside the castle before, though he was a native of Ferrara. As a child he had visited the Gonzaga winery. His father had worked there until his retirement. And the captain, like so many of the residents of the northern Italian city, had heard family stories of kinship with the original owners, the Estes. To him, it was merely something his relatives talked about on sweltering summer afternoons or blustery winter evenings when there was nothing else to do. Still, he was impressed with the splendor of the salon, and a bit embarrassed to have to ask personal questions of the castle's owner. He removed his hat and placed it on the mantel above the white marble fireplace, centering it carefully between a bronze clock with a beveled-glass front and gold-plated columns, and a Venetian glass vase in varigated shades of lavender.

Geoffredo stood next to him, resting one arm on the back of an empty wing chair that was upholstered in a satin needlepoint design.

Everyone assembled in the salon was introduced to the police captain by Geoffredo. Starting with the person seated nearest him, and in turn naming everyone around the room, the host began, "Signora Scalona, a friend from Florence . . . my brother Carlo, an artist from New York

147

... Fletcher Kimball, his friend, also from New York ... my brother's business manager, Samuel Hirschfeld, of the Hirschfeld Gallery in New York ... Murray Eastman, the husband of the unfortunate lady upstairs ... Teseo Gonzaga, my brother's stepdaughter, and Signore Eastman's granddaughter ... Signore Sassetti of the Galleria dell' Accademia in Florence ... Signorina Andrea Perkins, a restorer of art objects ... and Signora Sassetti."

None of the guests was asked to remain. But no one seemed motivated to leave.

They sat like strangers brought together by chance, carefully not looking at each other. Nor did they glance at their host or the police captain—that would seem a confession of morbid interest. Instead, most of them lifted their eyes no higher than the empty wing chair in front of Geoffredo.

The chair, under their solemn scrutiny, seemed to take on a presence. It was as though Death sat there like a relaxed, efficient accountant with an open ledger spread across his knees, in no hurry to disclose what discrepancy in the records had brought him there.

"First, the matter of the chef, Signore Gonzaga," the police captain said, taking a small cardboard-backed spiral notepad and a ballpoint pen from his pocket.

"Yes, of course." Geoffredo shook his head in bewilderment. "I've never known him to open a bottle of wine without being asked to do so. And I specifically told him I would decant the Sangiovese."

So far the captain's notes included only the information that both victims appeared to have died from drinking poisoned wine. Bottles that had contained the same vintage were found near each. Chemical analysis and the results of an autopsy that would have to be performed in the

148

police laboratory in Florence, he felt sure, would confirm his assumption.

"I know that sometimes after dinner," Geoffredo continued, "when a bottle that was not quite empty was returned to the kitchen, the chef finished off what was left. He thought that was his small secret. Though I knew, I didn't mind. But I have never known him to open a bottle just for himself."

"That may not have been the case this time, either," the captain said quietly, and made a notation on his spiral pad.

All the unopened bottles of Sangiovese on the cabinet had a lead seal around the cork. No similar seal was found near the body. That was the sort of detail that fascinated the captain and inspired him to search the plastic trash can under the sink. He had found a strip of lead there—at the bottom—beneath a full day's debris. The bottle had been opened quite some time before the chef sampled it.

"Where is the wine ordinarily kept?" The captain looked back at Geoffredo from his scribbled notes.

"In the wine cellar."

"And who brought the bottles up to the kitchen?"

"I did," Geoffredo answered. "I brought them up early this morning."

"Who else knew it was your plan to serve the wine this evening at dinner?"

"It certainly was no secret. It is well known that the Sangiovese is highly prized and served at special occasions."

"And this was such an occasion?"

"Yes. I had a small reception to honor my brother and his friends from New York, and . . ." Geoffredo glanced fleetingly at Andrea.

"And?"

Geoffredo shrugged. The fact that he had hoped to announce his engagement had no bearing on the questions
the policeman was asking. It was not, at any rate, something he chose to disclose at the moment. "And," he said,
"it also was an opportunity to display some newly restored
Renaissance miniature paintings."

"Ah." The captain nodded. Then he asked, "Were you
the only one with a key to the wine cellar?"

"No. It was necessary for several people to have access
. . . the chef, one or two people from the winery . . . others.
I could make a list . . ."

"Yes. That would be helpful. Perhaps later. And this
particular wine was bottled, when?"

"It was more than twenty years old."

The police captain paused a moment and retracted the
ballpoint pen, then pressed it open and retracted it again.

"Excuse me, Captain." Fletcher Kimball, still seated on
the floor, slowly opened his eyes and gazed toward the
front of the room. "My particular area of expertise is not a
detailed knowledge of the fruit of the vine, but is it possible for wine to turn toxic after being bottled such a long
time?"

"Certainly not!" It was Geoffredo who answered.
"Wines do not turn toxic under any circumstances."

"If that's the wine that was going to be served at dinner," Fletcher said in a lowered voice that only Carlo
standing next to him could hear, "I mean no disrespect to
Mrs. Eastman, but we should be grateful for the chef's
sneaky habits. Otherwise, we might all be trudging
through the golden corridor by this time."

For once, Carlo did not smile at Kimball's cynicism.

"Perhaps later," the police captain was saying to Geoffredo, "you will show me where the wine was stored in the
cellar. It had a special place?"

"Yes. The private reserve was kept separately. The back wall is fitted with diamond-shaped bins. Each bin holds twenty-four bottles, but the six I brought up this morning were the last ones left in that particular bin."

"And would it be obvious which group of bottles you would choose?"

"I suppose. It was . . . orderly . . . to take the bottles next in line."

"And that is what you did?"

"Yes."

"After the body of the chef was discovered—before I arrived, Signore Gonzaga—did it occur to you to inspect the remaining bottles in the kitchen?"

"No."

"No, of course not. Under the circumstances . . ."

"But I have the impression that they were still in the same spot on the cabinet where I put them this morning."

"And there was nothing obvious, nothing visible that would lead you to believe they had been tampered with? The original corks and seals seemed to be in place?"

"I couldn't tell you that without checking."

"I would be glad if you would do that for me later." The captain retracted the pen again and scratched his ear with it. "It would seem that the two bottles that had been opened were chosen at random."

Andrea watched the captain. What was he getting at? Did he think all six bottles were contaminated? How would that be possible when they were still corked and sealed? The only possibility she could imagine was if someone had injected poison into the bottle through the cork by using a long hypodermic needle. But wouldn't that be obvious? Wouldn't there be a hole left in the lead covering that would be easy to see?

The captain may have had the same thought. He crossed

to the bar at the side of the room and picked up a bottle of Bianco di Scandiano. It had been set out for the reception, but had not been needed and was still unopened. As the captain examined the wine he stood close enough to the couch where Andrea was seated with the Sassettis so that she, with no undue show of curiosity, could clearly see the top of the bottle, too. The cork had been completely covered with a lead seal that adhered to its shape, the rim of the bottle, and the top quarter of the neck. "These holes, Signore Gonzaga," the police officer pointed to four equally spaced tiny holes in the lead seal at the top of the bottle. "Why are they here?"

"That is so that the wine can breathe."

"It breathes," the captain inhaled audibly, "through the cork?"

"Yes. But, of course, not through lead. The lead is merely to hold the cork in place, and perforations must be left in it to allow the wine to oxidize."

No one would notice, Andrea thought, no one would ever know if a needle were inserted through one of the tiny holes in the seal.

The captain set the wine back on the bar and crossed the room again before he spoke. "And who actually took the wine to the cellar and placed it in the bins, Signore Gonzaga?"

"You mean when it was originally brought in from the winery?"

"Yes."

"That is impossible to say. The Sangiovese has not been moved since it was bottled and placed there. Probably the same procedure was used then as we use now. The wine is boxed in sequence when it comes out of the bottling room. Next, most of it is stored in the warehouse until it is delivered to our distributors. The bottles that are kept here in the castle are brought over by a *celleraro* and stacked in empty bins."

"Perhaps you would show me the cellar now," the captain said. Then, with a hint of embarrassment at directing the activities of the formally dressed group assembled in the salon, "There is no reason for your guests to remain here if they would prefer to go to their rooms."

"I have forgotten my responsibility as a host," Geoffredo said apologetically to the room in general. "You may be hungry. It is past time for dinner . . ." He stopped midsentence with the thought that the dinner they were to be served had been prepared by a man who now lay dead, and amended, "I will see that a cold buffet is served here in the salon."

At that moment one of the policemen the captain had assigned to search the grounds near the castle appeared in the doorway with a flashlight in one hand and a small paper sack in the other.

The captain motioned him into the room.

Geoffredo's guests, all but Murray Eastman and Tess, stood, and began to move about aimlessly. No one was hungry. No one seemed anxious to leave.

Andrea began to dismantle the display of the *tarocchi*, wrapping them individually in sheets of chamois and replacing them in the leather case. When she was almost finished, Carlo Gonzaga, with Fletcher Kimball trailing behind, appeared at her side.

"The seven of hearts." Carlo took one of the three remaining cards from the display rack and studied the miniature painting. It was of a young woman wearing a laurel wreath with a lyre in one hand and the lamp of knowledge in the other.

"This could be your card," Carlo said with a grin as he handed the *taroccho* to Andrea. "It means an educated

153

person . . . a scholar or professional. And if it were the first tarot card dealt to you, it would mean that you respond to requests for assistance and affection—both favorable and unfavorable."

"And what does that mean?" Andrea took the card from his hand and began to wrap it like the others.

"It could mean good news—or bad news."

"It sounds like the tarot reader is covered no matter what happens," Andrea said.

"It depends on which card follows the seven of hearts. It could indicate that your efforts are in the wrong direction, that your thoughts are wandering aimlessly, and that you're going around in circles. Isn't that right, Fletcher?"

Fletcher Kimball nodded. He closed his eyes in thought and said, "The favorable numbers that accompany the seven of hearts are five, forty-two, and ten. And the corresponding astrological sign is the Sun in one degree of Virgo."

Andrea replaced the seven of hearts in the ornate leather box and reached for the next to last card on the display. Carlo was holding it. He studied it a moment longer before giving it to Andrea.

"This one would seem to be for you and our Duchess Lucrezia. It's the *pettegolezzo*—gossip card."

In the miniature painting two young women had met in a road and were speaking seriously to each other. "Here, the divinatory meanings are hearsay and derogatory rumors. That unquestionably is a message to you from Lucrezia. She's telling you not to believe the lies told about her. And the reverse meaning is kinship and oneness. Didn't I tell you?" Carlo presented the card to Andrea with a knowing smile.

Fletcher Kimball added, "The favorable numbers are

four, thirteen, and sixty-one. Astrological signs are in the domain of Jupiter."

"Forget it, Carlo. You can't convert me," Andrea said indulgently. But she was only half-listening to Carlo and Kimball. She was much more interested in trying to hear what Geoffredo and the captain were discussing with the young policeman who had come in from outside.

The three men were standing with their heads close together. The captain's face was grim. Geoffredo looked bewildered.

"She may have been lying there all day." The uniformed man shifted the flashlight from one hand to the other. ". . . must have fallen and rolled beneath the clump of cypress . . . not visible from the path, only her hand . . ."

"This one is *Ladro*—thievery." Carlo handed her the last of the *tarocchi*, a painting of a thief sneaking into an open window. "The reverse meaning could be survival, rescue, or a just reward."

The policeman leaned over a small table in front of Geoffredo and the captain and began to empty the contents of the paper sack. When he straightened again, Andrea could see the red glass stem of a broken goblet that he had placed there.

". . . held between her thumb and forefinger," the policeman said, handing the stem to the captain. ". . . pieces of glass scattered around, and this . . ."

Before he could place it on the table, Geoffredo took the next exhibit from the policeman's hand. He held it up in front of his face to examine it more closely. "This looks like the overlay . . . it *is* a piece of the Borgia goblet that was kept on the shelf in the hall cabinet."

The voice of Fletcher Kimball droned on, "Ruled by Pisces, the domain of Jupiter and Water."

The captain took one last thing from the paper sack. Andrea could not see what he held in the palm of his hand.

After putting the piece of the goblet on the table next to the broken stem, Geoffredo turned to examine the last object.

Andrea was startled at his reaction. His back stiffened, and he turned quickly to look at her—at first accusingly, then simply without comprehension.

She put the last wrapped *taroccho* into the carved leather box and closed the lid, then took it to Geoffredo to replace it in the wall safe.

"It was on her finger," the policeman said. "It looked a bit grand for a temporary maid to be wearing, so I thought it was best to bring it here to you, sir."

"Do I understand what he is saying?" Geoffredo turned to the captain as though he needed confirmation from a second source. "Does he mean that this ring was found outside on the hand of a dead girl?"

Andrea stood frozen, staring at the garnet ring in the hand of the police captain. It was the ring worn by past Gonzaga countesses—the ring she had been certain was still in her evening bag.

Nineteen

Andrea felt like an unwitting participant in a sleight-of-hand performance. When she saw the police captain produce the garnet ring, her one thought was—it is not possible. If he had been a magician holding up her wristwatch—even though she saw it dangling from his fingers—she would not have believed it until her hand touched her bare wrist for confirmation. She felt the same disbelief now. Until she searched her beaded bag and confirmed that there was no longer anything wrapped inside the handkerchief, she was not fully convinced that the ring had been taken.

"Yes," she heard Geoffredo say, "yes, I recognize it. It is usually kept with other jewelry in the safe, but I took it out myself only today."

The policeman who had brought the ring in the paper sack with the broken piece of the glass goblet spoke softly to the captain. Andrea heard him say that he recognized the girl whose body he discovered concealed beneath the clump of cypress trees. He had known her since they were children, he said. Their mothers had worked side by side in the Gonzaga winery. Lately, the dead girl had been studying to be a cosmetician and sometimes worked for a domestic service as a temporary maid.

"I haven't known her well the last few years," he added hastily, then whispered something to the captain that Andrea could not hear.

A fleeting grin crossed the captain's face and was instantly replaced by a frown. He cleared his throat.

What was he thinking, Andrea wondered. Did he assume that the girl had stolen the ring? It had been stolen, all right, but by someone here in the salon. It had been taken from Andrea's beaded bag while she was upstairs with Carlo. Or maybe the policeman thought Geoffredo had given it to the girl—a present from the unmarried Count Gonzaga to the young hired girl from the domestic service. That would be a lively story to get started in Ferrara.

"Perhaps the ring should be returned to its place of safekeeping for now," the captain said to Geoffredo. "And later, if you would not mind signing a receipt . . . in case it should be needed as evidence."

"Of course."

"Geoffredo." Andrea hurried next to him and took his arm. She whispered close to his ear, "The ring was in my bag. It was on the table next to the *tarocchi* all evening."

Her proximity was more than Geoffredo could resist, and he put his arm around her waist briefly. "Don't worry yourself about it, *carissima*," he said softly, touching his lips to her hair.

No one else in the room could hear what was said, but Geoffredo's hurried embrace did not go unnoticed. The reaction of most of the guests was mild interest, but Carlo was amused, and Caterina was furious.

With consummate poise Caterina rose from her chair and unhurriedly crossed the room. Andrea had quickly put a space between herself and Geoffredo even before she realized that Rosa's cousin had come to fill it.

"You and this kind policeman must excuse me," Caterina said to Geoffredo as she wedged herself next to him. Smiling languidly, she traced the line of his jaw with a long graceful finger that then traveled down his chin and stopped briefly at his Adam's apple before curving inside the top of his collar. "I'll go on up to your apartment and wait for you, *mi amore*." She unhooked her finger from his shirt, kissed the tip of it and pressed it to Geoffredo's lips. "You must be so tired. Come up as soon as you can." She turned and walked through the salon to the vestibule as though she were leaving an empty room.

The police captain shifted his weight uncomfortably, looked at the floor, then back at Geoffredo. "Just a bit longer, signore. If we could go to the wine cellar now."

"Yes. Certainly." Geoffredo turned to his guests. "Please," he said to them, "conduct yourselves as you choose and forgive my absence."

Lucio Trotti quickly followed Geoffredo. "I might be of assistance if the captain wishes to see the winery."

"Yes, come with us if you don't mind," the captain answered.

Lucio stopped in front of the couch where Tess and Murray Eastman sat and tried to express his condolences. But giving up on his limited English, he gave Tess a quick kiss on the cheek instead.

She smiled a pale little smile, then took her grandfather's arm and led the still-dazed man toward the stairway and their rooms.

No one seemed interested in the antipasto, the cold

sliced pork and cheeses, and the crusty bread that had been spread out on the serving table. Conspicuously absent was any variety of Gonzaga wines. Instead, there were bottles of mineral water.

Rosa and Vittorio Sassetti soon said affectionate good-nights to Andrea and went to the second floor and the accommodations that had been prepared for them.

Now only Andrea, Carlo, and his two satellites—Fletcher Kimball and Sammy Hirschfeld—were left in the salon.

"One moment, Miss Perkins," Sammy Hirschfeld said as Andrea started to follow the Sassettis from the room. "I want to compliment you again on your presentation this evening."

"Thank you." Andrea started again to leave.

"Just one more second, if you don't mind. There is something I would like to discuss with you." Sammy paused and, with an amiable expression to match his tone of voice, said, "If Count Gonzaga agrees to let me show the *tarocchi* in America, I'd like to work out a national tour and perhaps have you accompany the display. Do you think you might be available? I know this is not a good time to talk business, but—"

"You're right, Mr. Hirschfeld. This is not a good time."

"Forget it, Sammy," Carlo said.

"But she'd be perfect. No one knows more about Bonifacio Bembo and the history of the cards."

"I don't doubt that Miss Perkins would be a bigger attraction than the miniatures." Carlo shoved a hand through his unruly hair, then jumped to his feet, stretched, and sauntered toward the doorway. "But Geoffredo will never let you get your hands on the *tarocchi*."

"Sammy, sometimes your timing is atrocious," Fletcher

Kimball chimed in peevishly. "Can't you see what this poor girl's been through tonight? What we've *all* been through."

"If you were to ask him, Carlo . . ."

"He won't let you take the miniatures on tour. He'll keep them here. He may never let them be shown at all."

"Good night, gentlemen," Andrea said.

They all followed her into the vestibule. The brass and crystal chandelier that was suspended by a chain from the skylight on the third floor had been turned out. Only the backlights behind the statues were still on and gave the marble figures an even more forbidding appearance than usual.

"You know who the servants will blame for the poisoned wine," Carlo said casually to Andrea as they started up the stairs. Then darkly, dramatically, "Lucrezia. Who else— they will ask each other—could it have been?"

Andrea did not answer him.

"And not just the servants, the whole city of Ferrara, when word of the *tragedia delle Gonzaga* gets out." Then, as though he were discussing nothing of more consequence than the number of steps on the stairway, he added, "Even the police. They're all home grown. Oh, it may show up on the captain's report as 'death by poisoning from an unknown source.' But the verdict will be 'death at the hands of Duchess Lucrezia Borgia d'Este.' "

"Carlo, that is hardly an appropriate topic of conversation, either." Sammy Hirschfeld's words were polite and apologetic. He was practiced in smoothing over his clients' abrasiveness.

"This is important for her to know," Carlo persisted, finding his monologue amusing and typically not caring how anyone else responded. "Who but Lucrezia had such a practiced hand at poisoning? And for corroborating evidence, there was the snow. Snow in late spring always brings disaster. Everyone in Ferrara knows that. Then there's the ring—the way it mysteriously turned up on that girl's finger." Carlo leaped the last step and stood facing Andrea at the head of the second-floor hallway. "You *were* the last one to have the ring in your possession, were you not?" He grinned at her like a naughty child.

Andrea stopped, too. Enough, she thought. That was enough of Carlo Gonzaga. There was nothing amusing about him now. With no regret—in fact, with pleasure— she swung a fist at him with all her strength and hit him on the left cheek.

Even if this had been his idea of a joke, she had grown sick of Carlo's persistence that she was Lucrezia Borgia reincarnate. But she might have ony slapped instead of slugged him if the need to strike out had not been building inside her all day.

Lying on the surface was her sense of injustice at the three unnatural, unexplained deaths. Beneath that was her regret about Geoffredo; she was sorry she could not return his feelings and dreaded having to tell him. Deeper still, she realized, was an ache that had hollowed out a hole inside her, an emptiness left by Aldo Balzani.

She had not known she would feel this way about the chief of detectives of the Florentine Police Department when she let him walk out the door of the Este Hotel this morning. And she had not said a word that would bring him back.

Well, she wanted him here, now. She needed his strength and protection. He could straighten out the absurdity of the poisoning. He could explain to Geoffredo that she was not available. And he could have bloodied Carlo Gonzaga's nose.

She was surprised to see that she had taken care of Carlo's nose herself.

Groaning, he pressed his hand against his upper lip, then pulled it away and stared at his bloody fingers. "Lady, I think you must have spent one lifetime as an Amazon," he said without rancor as he reached in his pocket for a handkerchief.

"You had that coming," Sammy Hirschfeld said.

"You do go a bit too far." Fletcher Kimball handed Carlo his own handkerchief as a spare.

Carlo ignored Hirschfeld. It was unproductive to have a meaningless disagreement with his business manager. A fair percentage of the artist's success depended upon the goodwill and enthusiasm of Sammy Hirschfeld.

But Fletcher Kimball was different. He was in Italy as a guest in the Gonzaga Castle only because of Carlo's whim and open checkbook. "What do you mean, 'a bit far'?" Carlos snapped at the astrologer.

"Three people are dead here."

"What am I supposed to do about it?"

"At a time of grief . . ." Fletcher Kimball shrugged.

"Grief?" Carlo's nose hurt. He was beginning to get angry.

"One of the dead *was* your mother-in-law," Sammy Hirschfeld said in a rare defense of Fletcher Kimball.

"Harriet Eastman hated my guts. She would not have been grief-stricken to see me dead." Carlo combed his free hand through his unruly hair. "Besides, Harriet would have drunk herself to death anyway. The poisoned wine just made it quicker and cleaner."

Andrea was surprised, but not sorry that she had hit Carlo. Without an apology she went into her room and closed the door behind her, shutting out the voices, shutting in the silence.

Twenty

The fourth murder that night might never have happened if there had been an apparent pattern to the previous three. But what could possibly have linked together the chef, the temporary maid, and Harriet Eastman? Why were they killed? What did they have in common? Perhaps, nothing—or at least nothing that would ever be discovered. And that was the intriguing part of it all to one of the people who was there that evening at the Castello di Gonzaga.

It was a sudden realization that death was incredibly simple—and such an easy answer to certain problems. It was the sort of insight that made the person wonder why murder had never presented itself as a solution before.

Andrea was glad to leave Carlo and his disagreeable friends, but the prospect of being alone was hardly more pleasant.

Her room seemed larger, colder, and more impersonal than ever before.

After tonight, she decided, there was no reason for her

to stay in Ferrara. The fresco was still not even started, but it had been on the wall of the castle for nearly five hundred years. It could wait a little longer—until Geoffredo's guests had gone back to New York.

Sleep was out of the question. She undressed, but did not even consider going to bed. Instead of a nightgown, she pulled on a pair of jeans and a turtleneck sweater. Having made the decision to leave, she spread her suitcase open on the window seat and began to pack.

The icy wind tapped the window against the ledge and scattered the powdery snow across the inside sill. Andrea tried to fasten the latch, but it would not close easily. The problem was, she discovered, that the lower hinge had been circled and clamped partway open by one of the wild vines that climbed and clung to the castle wall. Growing from it and frozen against the pane were two leaves, like open hands with webbed fingers reaching to come in. Andrea shivered, not just from the cold. She decided to let the suitcase wait until morning.

It was not just rationalization, she told herself, that sent her out of the room and down to her own friendly clutter in the studio. It was a practical decision. After all, her equipment had to be packed, too.

The police captain said, "Lucrezia used arsenic, isn't that so?" He and Geoffredo and Lucio Trotti were making their way single file down the narrow stairs to the wine cellar. It was slow going for the captain. The cold weather irritated his arthritis. "As I recall, she had a collection of rings with concealed compartments that held the poison, and her method was to sprinkle equal parts of arsenic and sugar on top of fresh fruit, which she served to unsuspecting enemies. Or so the story goes."

Geoffredo answered with an Italian saying that often

followed old wives' tales. *"Se non e' vero 'e ben trovato."* Even if it is not true, it is a good invention.

Geoffredo was grateful to slip back into his native language with the two Italian men. Speaking only English to Andrea and Carlo's guests had been something of a strain.

At the bottom of the stairs, Geoffredo flipped the master switch that turned on the lights at both ends of each row of floor-to-ceiling bins. Above each of the diamond-shaped alcoves was a small sign that stated the variety of wine and the vintage. Most of the bins held two dozen bottles. Geoffredo led the way to the back wall, where the remaining Sangiovese di Romagna was stored and pointed out the bin he had emptied of its last six bottles that morning.

The three men stood looking seriously at the empty space that told them nothing. The captain would instruct an assistant to check for fingerprints, though he had little hope that evidence of any importance could be found in the cellar. Too many people had access. As soon as he was back upstairs he would call the police station in Florence and request the services of a scientific specialist. More sophisticated methods might yield some useful information. But for now, all the captain could think to do was ask the same polite questions any visitor would ask: how was the temperature maintained, what was the capacity for storage, how old was the oldest vintage, who arranged the bottles, who removed them? He did not make written notes of any of the answers. But there must be something, something here that was significant.

"This logbook may be of interest." Geoffredo led the other two men to a poorly lit desk in the corner. "Records have been kept for several hundred years." He opened a large volume that was lined horizontally and divided vertically into columns. "The variety and number of bottles brought in is always recorded, and notations are made when they are removed. Here are my initials." Geoffredo pointed to the open page where the removal of the lethal wine was recorded.

What good was that, the captain thought. He already knew it was Geoffredo who had selected the wine.

"Yes, it's a very nice book," the captain said, "nice straight columns." He turned again toward the stairs, dreading the climb back up with his sore knee.

"Is there anything else down here you would like to see?"

"I think not. But if you would show me where the wine is bottled?"

"Signore Trotti might be of more assistance there. That's really his province," Geoffredo said.

"If I can assist in any way . . ." Lucio lifted his open palms to show his sincerity.

"Are there poisons kept on the premises? Rat poison, insecticides, that sort of thing?"

"Yes, of course," Geoffredo answered. "It is necessary to use insecticides in the vineyards, otherwise it would be the bugs and beetles that harvested the grapes."

"And where are they kept, the poisons?"

"There is a shed especially for that purpose between here and the winery. Lucio, will you show him?"

Lucio nodded.

"If there is nothing further . . ."

"Not this evening, Signore Gonzaga. Tomorrow, yes."

"About Signora Eastman, and the chef, and that unfortunate girl. Where will they stay?" Geoffredo could not bring himself to refer to their demise. It was as though they were overflow guests and he was inquiring about alternate hotel arrangements.

"One of my men has called for a conveyance to take them to Ferrara. You need not be present when it arrives."

The captain held onto the handrail as the three men climbed the stairs. When they reached the rear hallway, he said, "The phone, signore . . . I will find it in the kitchen?"

"Yes. Just inside the door."

"Grazie!"

"Arrivederci."

As Geoffredo started up the second flight toward his apartment, the captain glanced in that direction. Standing on the first landing was Caterina Scalona in a silk print dressing gown with a matching belt looped at the waist.

"I'm glad the captain has finally finished with you," she said, smoothing out a fold in the soft fabric. "It must have been such a trying day."

Geoffredo inhaled deeply, as though he were fortifying himself for another unpleasant task. Then, remembering his obligation as a host, he said, "Lucio, see that a case of wine of the captain's choice is delivered to his home." The offer was made out of habit. It was the usual conclusion to a visit by a VIP. But, remembering what had brought the police to the Castello di Gonzaga, Geoffredo added, "At some future time . . . in more amenable circumstances."

Andrea fastened several small paintbrushes together with a rubber band and dropped them into a canvas bag. She heard the three men talking in the back hall, but left her studio door closed, not wishing to interrupt—or be interrupted. A few minutes later there was a knock from outside.

"Signorina Perkins, isn't it?" The captain gave her a small bow and a large smile.

"Yes."

"You have just been in my conversation with a gentleman at the police station in Florence."

"Oh?" She drew in her breath, waiting for what he would say, knowing he must mean he had been talking with Aldo Balzani.

"My friend, the captain of detectives, sends you his regards. He also gave me instructions, and a message for you that he says you are to follow without question."

"He's pretty bossy, isn't he?" Andrea grinned. Suddenly the policeman from Ferrara was an old friend. Someone she could talk with about Aldo Balzani. "What is this important message?"

"I called him to arrange for the assistance of an expert from his laboratory, and naturally, I told him of the unfortunate events here this evening. His first question was not, 'How many are dead?' or, 'Has an arrest been made?' He asked first, 'Is Andrea Perkins all right?'"

Andrea could not have stopped the smile that spread across her face.

"When I assured him that you were in excellent condition when I saw you last, he insisted that I assign one of my men to keep a special eye on you until he got here."

"He's coming here?"

"I would think that he has already left. And since I have arranged to tour the winery with Signor' Trotti, and cannot have the pleasure of protecting you myself, I will track down one of my men and have him come to stay with you."

"That's really not necessary, Captain."

"Ah! I insist. My old friend Aldo would never forgive me, otherwise."

"But I'm sure your men have more important things . . ."

"No. It must be as Aldo says. Unless you would care to come with me to the winery."

"I think I will," Andrea said. "To tell you the truth, I'd like to get out of the castle for a while."

The captain, in a fatherly manner, advised her to button her coat and wear a scarf if she had one. "It is quite cold for March."

Lucio Trotti was waiting for them near the rear exit. Andrea greeted him and fell easily into conversation with him in Italian.

The captain absently tapped his ballpoint pen against an aluminum pole supporting the awning above the sidewalk as they passed. The minor motion dislodged a small clump of snow that had collected on the scalloped overhang. Icy crystals blew apart in midair, flying and falling like tiny moths in the yellow circle of light from an outside standard, then came to rest again on an uneven patch of frozen grass.

"You asked to see where the insecticides were kept, Captain. It might be more convenient to go there first."

The shed was about equal in distance from the castle and the winery. Lucio led the way across a gravel path to a wooden building about the size of a garage. The door was painted red. Above it was a spotlight that clearly illuminated a large sign: *Pericolo—Ingresso Vietato*. Danger—Keep Out.

"Naturally, we keep the shed locked," Lucio said.

"Will you open it, please?"

Lucio felt in both the front pockets of his dress trousers, then the outside and breast pockets of his suit jacket. "These are not the clothes I work in," he said. "Usually I dress like the other workers." Then, a bit shamefacedly, Lucio reached on top of the molding above the door and took down a key. "It is not generally known that this is kept here," he said hurriedly. "Only by those who are directly responsible for dispensing the insecticides."

"Umm." The captain looked grim and shook his head.

The key might as well have been hung from a hook beneath the doorknob, Andrea thought.

Lucio unlocked the door and turned on a light. The floor was gravel. Three walls were lined with shelves that contained well-labeled boxes and bottles and jars. A long wooden rack with protruding pegs was attached to the front wall. Hanging from the pegs were three rubberized sets of coveralls with drawstring ties at the ankles, wrists, and neck. They were bright orange, as were the accompanying brimmed hats with plexiglass coverings for the face and back of the head. Three pair of rubberized gloves were spread neatly on a nearby bench.

"Those are the protective uniforms worn by the men who handle the insecticides," Lucio explained, then called the captain's attention to a large chart on the inside of the door. Listed there were the substances in the boxes and containers.

Andrea looked quickly at the list. Most of them had abbreviations for their unpronounceable technical names. An explanatory paragraph provided by the manufacturer was included at the top of the posted page:

> Cholinesterase inhibitors are used in agriculture for the control of soft-bodied insects. They consist of two distinct chemical groups of compounds: organophosphorus derivatives and carbamates. In both groups there are widely varying toxicities. Those listed below may be used to prepare dusts and wettable powders to be used in factories and fields. Follow printed instructions exactly!

Those listed were:

> Aspon—(tetra-n-propyl dithionopyrophosphate)
> Folex—(tributyl phosphorotrithiote)

Nem-A-Tak—(fosthietane)
TEPP—(tetraethyl pyrophosphate)
Vam—(Vamidothion)

The captain took out his spiral notepad, his pen poised.
"And all of these insecticides are poisonous to humans?"

"Not all of them. Some would only make you nauseated.
But, yes, some could kill you."

"Would you make a list of the most dangerous ones for
me, Lucio?"

"In my office is a copy of the list that is posted. I will
mark it for you."

"That would be helpful. Now, if we could see the winery," the captain said, starting in that direction.

Lucio locked the shed and hurried in front of the captain, leading the way. "I am embarrassed about the key,"
he said. "You must think we are careless, which is not true.
Our safety record is excellent. When the shed was built,
the Town Council presented Signore Gonzaga with a certificate commending him on his concern for the welfare of
his workers."

"How long ago was that?"

"Several years, perhaps twenty, when I was still a boy
working in the fields."

"And where were the poisons kept before then?"

"In a closet, next to the supply room in the winery."

"And how did it happen that the shed was built and
Signore Gonzaga received his admirable certificate?"

The path was dark, and neither of the men could see
Andrea smile. She liked the police captain. His manner
was courteous and courtly, but his questions were often
tinged with irony.

"There had been one accident," Lucio admitted.

"A serious accident?"

"A woman died. But as I said," Lucio hurried on, "that was years ago."

"Perhaps, however, you still remember. Will you tell me about it?"

"A woman in the bottling room was poisoned."

"Poisoned? How?"

"She came in contact with some TEPP, one of the insecticides used to control fruit flies."

Andrea had meant to stay silent, but it seemed uncharacteristic of Geoffredo to allow such gross carelessness. She said, "How could that happen? Did she eat some unwashed grapes?"

"Somehow the insecticide got on her hands."

"And then onto something she was eating?" the captain asked.

"No. TEPP doesn't have to be ingested," Lucio said. "It's the most powerful poison we use. It penetrates the skin and is lethal within minutes. That is what all the rubberized gear and heavy gloves were for in the insecticide shed. All my men are cautioned never to handle any of the poisons without full-body protection."

"I still don't understand," Andrea said. "How did the woman die?"

"No one ever knew."

They had reached the entrance to the winery. Lucio buzzed an outside bell, and in a few seconds a sleepy looking guard opened the heavy oak door. He nodded to the three of them, then went back inside a small glassed-in office where the only light was from the screen of a small television set.

Lucio turned on the lights in the reception room. "The official explanation of her death, or so the story goes, was that she had seen a rat and thought she was dishing out rat poison. A small amount of the powder was found around her work station, where she had apparently spilled it." Lucio laughed halfheartedly. "But naturally, when there was a poisoning at the Castello di Gonzaga there was only one person to be blamed . . ."

"Not Lucrezia again," Andrea said.

"Ah, signorina. The stories that are told. The captain knows them . . ."

The captain agreed that he did.

"And," Lucio went on, "the woman who died had claimed for many years that she was the rightful heir to the castle."

Andrea pulled her hair out from under her collar and untied the scarf the captain had insisted she wear. "Another Este relative?"

Lucio nodded. "But this one, it seems, was more vocal than most. She was constantly threatening to take the Gonzagas to court whenever she was unhappy at work."

The reception room looked as though it had been furnished by a decorator with a particular fondness for ferns and comfortable rustic furniture fashioned from old wine kegs. On the wall facing the front door was a photographic mural of the vineyards with the castle in the background.

"Was there something specific that you wanted to see in the winery, Captain?" Lucio asked.

"Nothing in particular. Just pretend that we are important visitors and take us on a tour."

Lucio motioned them through a hallway and down a flight of metal steps.

It was not true, Andrea thought, that the captain was looking for nothing in particular in the winery. He was looking for nothing at all. He barely glanced around him, and seemed interested only in asking questions of Lucio.

"The girl we found beside the path to the servants' quarters. It was you who identified her, my officer said."

"Yes."

"Did you know her well?"

"No. But I knew she had been hired to help out with the dinner and reception this evening."

"And did you find her agreeable?"

Andrea lagged behind, making a show of inspecting an automated conveyor belt on the assembly line so as not to embarrass Lucio or inhibit the captain.

"What do you mean, agreeable?" Lucio stopped and looked sharply at the captain.

"I am not accusing you of anything," the captain said blandly. "I simply meant, she was nice—was she not? Did you like her?"

"I hardly knew her," Lucio said. "But if anything, I suppose I felt sorry for her."

"Why was that?"

"She seemed so . . . ambitious. She was not content with her life and was always trying to better herself. There was little opportunity for that in this province."

"Did you know of her, uh, reputation?"

"Ferrara is not a large city, Captain."

The captain professed to have an interest in the process of crushing and pressing the grapes and asked appropriate questions about how they were fermented. After a moment of silence, he said, "Had you ever seen her at the castle before?"

"Who?" Lucio was not convincing in his supposed lapse of memory.

"The girl, Lucio. The dead girl."

"Not that I recall."

"Would it be possible that she was acquainted with Signore Gonzaga's brother or his friends?"

"I suppose it's possible. The people from New York had

been here several days. The girl may have been hired to assist in the kitchen for the length of their stay. I do not ordinarily dine at the castle, Captain, so I wouldn't know."

"The winery seems to have quite modern equipment," Andrea said to confirm her interest in the physical facility and lack of curiosity about what the two men were discussing.

"Would you care to see the refrigerated tanks for controlled fermentation of white wines?" Lucio asked. "Signor' Gonzaga is very proud of them." He pointed to a catwalk that led to a platform above the huge vats.

"Tomorrow, perhaps," the captain answered. As if the cold weather weren't enough to play hell with his knee, there were all these stairs. "I think this is enough of a tour for one evening. We're all tired, are we not?" The captain patted Lucio on the back. "And maybe a little upset, huh?"

Lucio stiffened and drew back. "Why do you say that?"

"You forget your keys . . . you can not remember the dead girl we are discussing . . ." The captain smiled at Andrea and motioned that she should precede him back to the reception room. "Forgive me, Lucio, I am an old policeman. For me, three deaths is upsetting. It may be that young managers of wineries are made of sturdier stuff."

When they were back inside the castle, Lucio left the other two and went toward his apartment near the servants' quarters.

"What do you think of that young man," the captain asked Andrea when Lucio was gone.

"He seems . . . nice. He was really rather touching with Murray Eastman and his granddaughter in the salon."

"Signore Eastman is wealthy?"

"I suppose."

"And I can see for myself the granddaughter is pretty."

"You're a rascal." Andrea laughed. "Don't you believe anyone?"

"I believe my friend Aldo when he says I am to protect you. I must wait for the ambulance. But before that, I will see you to your room."

"I have a better idea. Come in my studio and I'll make us a cup of tea."

There were two chairs in Andrea's studio, an armless typing chair she used at the worktable, and a straight-backed wooden chair she offered to the captain. She dropped tea bags into two mismatched mugs, and filled them with boiling water when the tea kettle whistled on the hot plate.

The captain accepted a mug and thanked her, balancing his hat on one crossed knee. "We must always wait," he said with a sigh. "We must wait to have other people help us. Until the man from the lab makes his examination, there is no way to know what the poison was, or how it got inside the bottles."

Andrea perched on the edge of the worktable and put her feet in the seat of the typing chair. She cupped her hands around a garish mug she had bought from a vendor in Assisi. "Captain, I was wondering earlier . . . would it be possible, do you suppose, to inject the poison into the bottle with a hypodermic needle?"

"An examination of the cork may tell."

She sipped at the hot, bitter tea. "Sorry there's no sugar."

The captain waved his hand politely, as though sugar was the last thing he would ever want.

How else could the poison have gotten there, Andrea wondered. Could the seals have been removed and re-placed so expertly that it was not apparent to the naked eye? But, maybe the poison was not in the bottle at all, she thought suddenly. She set the mug down beside her and leaned forward. "Maybe it was the glasses that were poisoned," she began, and then remembered. "No, the glass the girl used didn't even come from the kitchen. She took it from the antique cabinet in the hall."

"And Signora Eastman used a glass from the bathroom," the captain reminded her.

"It's obvious that not all of those three people were killed intentionally. Who would want them dead? And how could anyone know they would drink the wine?"

The captain leaned back and closed his eyes. "Tonight was a special occasion, was it not? Signore Gonzaga would have raised a toast to his brother and his friends. Who would have been the first to actually taste the wine?"

"Geoffredo, I suppose. He was the host."

"So he would have taken the first swallow . . . or made it appear that he did."

Andrea looked up sharply at the captain, but he did not enlarge on his speculation. She realized it was his responsibility to be suspicious of everyone, but she could not believe Geoffredo was capable of such an act.

"There was no smell of almonds in the kitchen," the captain said, as though to himself.

"You're thinking of cyanide," Andrea said. Then, answering the captain's surprised look, "I have to know something about poisons. I use a lot of chemicals and poisonous substances in my work."

"I see. One should beware of a pretty lady who knows about poison." The captain smiled and took a sip of tea to show that he was teasing her. Seriously, he said, "No. Cyanide would have acted as quickly as did the poisoned wine, but there was not the telltale scent of almonds near any of the bodies."

"And arsenic can be ruled out . . ."

"Yes, it takes too long." The captain uncrossed his legs and put his hat on the floor, then leaned back against the wall, balancing his chair on the two back legs. "It could be that the poisoner did not know what the substance was himself . . . simply that it came from a container marked 'poison.' "

"My God! An insecticide. Do you think that's what it was?"

"Again, we must wait," he said. "The laboratory will identify the substance. But we may learn that it was an exotic bug killer."

"Of course. Whoever he was, the man must have grabbed a handful of something from the shed . . ."

"Or the woman."

"I suppose it could have been." She wondered if he were thinking of anyone in particular. The first woman who came to Andrea's mind was Caterina Scalona. Caterina tried to disguise her jealousy, but that was something one woman could not easily hide from another. Caterina knew that Geoffredo would be the first to drink the wine. Would she have tried to kill him just because she was afraid he was losing interest in her? Maybe. But it was impossible! She had not even been at the castle when the temporary girl opened the first bottle. And that ruled out Rosa Sassetti, too, because they had come from Florence together. As though Rosa could ever be suspected of doing anything more sinister than insisting you have second and third servings of her pasta malnatti. If you ruled out Harriet Eastman and the possibility of accidental death or suicide, that left only Tess Gonzaga, and Andrea herself.

She looked at the captain, but his eyes were closed and his face told her nothing. After a moment she said, "But there's still the question of how the poison got into the bottle."

"*When*, I think, is more important." The captain's eyes flew open, and his chair teetered on one leg before the other three hit the floor. "When was it put in the bottle. This morning? Last week? Or long before that. It might be that it was nothing so involved as using a hypodermic needle or replacing the cork and seal. What could be easier than putting the poison in the bottle when it came down the assembly line?"

"But that was more than twenty years ago."

"The label will tell us. We could track it to the day and the hour in the fine record book in the Gonzaga wine cellar."

"The woman Lucio told us about!"

"A rat may not have been her intended victim, after all."

"And she used an insecticide—like TEPP—not knowing that merely holding it in her hand would kill her, too."

"One must wait to see if that could be the case."

"If it is," Andrea said, "no one will ever know whom she meant to kill."

"Oh, yes. I can tell you now."

"Who?"

"Anyone." The captain sighed deeply, then drank the rest of his tea. "Anyone who was privileged to drink the private reserve of the Gonzaga family. Anyone. Anytime. It did not matter. She was an Este."

"Or claimed to be—like half of Ferrara, from what I have heard."

"It is true that the Estes were generous in sowing their seed. And though they could not give their name to as many of their offspring as they would have liked, they were always willing to acknowledge them without shame."

"But surely no one still believes that it would be possible for an Este to reclaim the Gonzaga castle and winery. Maybe a hundred or two hundred years ago, but . . ."

"But not in the twentieth century?" The captain smiled sadly. "Ah, signorina, what Lucio Trotti said about the young temporary girl who died here today is true of so many of our young people. They want to better themselves. They want more—not just wealth—they want the glory they have heard of from the past. We in Italy know what we have been. Our ancestors once walked among such men as Cosimo Medici, Galileo, Leonardo, and Michelangelo. Now, the men we hear of are terrorists, communists, and petty black marketeers. How would the present be bearable without the thoughts of our glorious past?"

"I suppose it's possible."

"I think we will find that in this case, the murderer died long before her victims."

Andrea considered what he had said. "There's really nothing new about random killing, is there? It's just done on a larger scale these days. In Japan there were poisoned candy bars put on the shelves in supermarkets, and in America, there were the contaminated pain pills. But in both of those instances, the poisoners demanded huge ransoms from the manufacturing companies."

"Money is only one motive for murder. In Italy, revenge has always been more popular." The captain stood and stretched. "And it's possible that the woman may simply have been insane."

A dog on the grounds of the castle was first to hear the siren and barked energetically. As the faint metallic scream came closer, it was thoughtfully cut off by the driver. There was no traffic to warn and no hurry to arrive.

"The ambulance is here. I must go now," the captain said. "But first, I will see you safely to your room."

"There's really no need."

"I promised Aldo," he said, taking her by the arm.

It was useless to protest. Andrea let herself be led up the back stairs. At the door to her room she thanked the captain and went inside.

What he had said must be true. What other explanation could there be?

It was not until she heard the ambulance back up closer to the castle and the gurney rolling across the gravel that she remembered the ring.

Twenty-one

Andrea had promised the police captain that she would lock herself in her room. She would have if there had been a key. There were cut crystal knobs the size of paper-weights on each side of the door, and a keyhole large enough to stick a thumb in, but no key. However, even if she had built a barricade using all the heavy cherry wood furniture, she doubted it would have kept Caterina Scalona out. As it was, with nothing to stop her, when Caterina flung open the door, it was as though the room imploded.

She stood rigid a moment, framed in the doorway. She had changed back into the green silk dress she had worn when she arrived. The mink stole was thrown loosely across her shoulders. Taking in the whole room at one glance, her eyes narrowed and fastened on Andrea, who stood over an open suitcase at the window seat. Caterina held the pose a moment longer, then raised her right arm straight out and sighted down her index finger at Andrea. The movement of her shoulder sent the cape slipping to the floor. Without glancing down, Caterina kicked the cape behind her into the hallway and came into the room.

Andrea had seen *Medea* at La Scala, but the staging could not compare with this.

"You think he will marry you, eh?" Her voice was like a contralto chorus speaking in unison. "Never! Not as long as he lives!"

Andrea felt at a disadvantage, if for no other reason than costuming. She was in her stocking feet and was forced to look up at the other woman who wore four-inch heels. "Look, Caterina . . . I am here as an employee . . ."

"Ha! An employee!"

"I was hired by Geoffredo . . ."

"Hired!"

"You saw the exhibition of the *tarocchi* in the salon."

"Yes! I saw the exhibition in the salon!"

"If you got the wrong idea . . ."

"There was no wrong idea. I asked Carlo. He told me Geoffredo was going to marry you."

"Carlo doesn't know anything about it."

"Ah, but when I asked Geoffredo if it was true, he admitted it!"

Andrea tried to soften the encounter and said in as close to a rational voice as possible, "This has been a terrible day for all of us. No one can be expected to behave in a normal way under the circumstances."

"There is one thing only that I have to tell you." Caterina's long neck stretched and she lowered her chin so that she was looking down on the top of Andrea's head. "There will never be another Countess Gonzaga until I decide to get a divorce and marry Geoffredo myself."

It was stubbornness more than anything else that kept Andrea from telling Caterina that she had no intention of marrying him. But she had not even had an opportunity to tell Geoffredo that yet, and in fairness, she was not going to break the news to Caterina first. She said, "It seems to me it's up to Geoffredo to decide who he wants to marry."

"The decision is made. He will marry no one else."

Caterina pivoted on the balls of her feet and in four graceful strides reached the door, opened it, and turned again. "And if you are wondering what happened to this," she held her hand out straight, and Andrea saw the garnets glowing on the middle finger of her left hand. "This is where Lucrezia's ring will stay forever." She flipped the catch open with the thumbnail of her right hand. "It's no more difficult to solve problems today than it was when this ring was first worn."

Caterina turned again and in a fluid motion scooped up the mink cape from the hallway just as Geoffredo appeared behind her. She flung the fur over her shoulder, then clutching the front of his shirt with the ringed hand said, with her face only inches from his, "You can believe me, *mi amore*, this girl will never be your bride." She released him, took a step to the side and walked around him and down the hall.

"Andrea, *carissima*." Looking stricken, Geoffredo said in Italian, "I would give my eyes," then in English, "I would not have had this happen to you. The ring was on my dresser. She took it without my knowing."

"Geoffredo, I don't want the ring."

"Please forgive. Understand that no one can change my intentions toward you." Then in delayed anger he threw his hands in the air, "She is so *drammatico*!"

"We have to discuss this."

"*Domani*, my sweet." He must have known that at that moment Andrea would refuse him. Tomorrow he might be able to change her mind.

"I'm leaving tomorrow."

"Try to rest." It was as though he had not heard her. "When this night is gone the world will be normal again.

We will talk in the morning." He blew her a kiss and quietly closed the door behind him.

The whole scene seemed to be stolen from Euripides. Andrea was exhausted. She lay down on the bed. Several minutes later she heard the rich hum of the Ferrari's engine, the efficient shifting of gears, and the clatter of gravel. As the sound became distant, a heavier vehicle started up—the ambulance. It left at a slower pace, but soon the only sound was the barking of the dog near the far gate. He had not had such an exciting evening in a long time.

There were so many questions still to be answered. The captain's theory about the poisoned wine had been convincing. But there was still the question of the ring. Though Caterina had it now, Andrea could not believe that it was she who had stolen it from the beaded bag in the salon and put it on the finger of the dead girl. That was not Caterina's style.

And there was the fire that afternoon in the back hall of the castle. Andrea would have been less surprised if that had been Caterina's doing, though she suspected that if Caterina started the fire she would have made a better job of it and burned the castle down. As much as she would have liked to blame the other woman, it was not possible. At the time the fire was discovered, Caterina was on the autostrada driving Rosa and Vittorio to Ferrara from Florence.

But the ring was the biggest puzzle, partly because Andrea felt responsible for its loss. She should never have left it in her handbag unattended. The ring should have been returned to the safe with the *tarocchi*.

Suddenly her eyes flew open and she sat straight up.

Were the *tarocchi* in the safe?

She tried to remember when she had last seen the antique tarot cards. They had been packed away in the leather box and she had meant to hand them to Geoffredo. But it was at that moment that she saw the garnet ring in the police captain's hand for the first time. And after that, she had no memory of the Bonifacio Bembo miniatures.

Surely Geoffredo had locked them in the safe. But was he as stunned as she? Would he have thought to do that with the news of three deaths coming so quickly—deaths that had apparently been caused by wine from his own cellar?

The box could still be sitting on the makeshift bar in the salon for all she knew.

She got up and slipped on her tennis shoes, breaking a string in her hurry, and having to tie a knot in it.

It was late, maybe close to dawn. The question of the *tarocchi*, at least, could be answered by simply going down to the salon to check. She crept as quietly as possible into the hall. Her footsteps made no noise in the wide marble corridor. All the doors on both sides were closed. The only light she could see was a diffused glow where the stairway curved down to the vestibule.

As she grew closer, strangely, the light grew dimmer and flickered. It was not until she reached the top of the stairs that she smelled smoke.

The vestibule was three stories high. From the floor of the entry, it extended up past the top of the curved stairway on the second floor to a sort of mezzanine on the third with only one exit that led to Geoffredo's apartment.

The smoke was coming from the first-floor entry and funneled upward to an opening in the domed skylight. From where Andrea was, the smell was faint. The smoke was thickest around the mezzanine.

Andrea ran down the stairs. A wine crate, like the one that had burned outside her studio, smoldered harmlessly in the middle of the marble floor.

It was as though the fire had been started for the sole purpose of attracting attention. But unless someone happened upon it accidentally, as Andrea had, the smoke would not have been noticed except by someone in Geoffredo's third-floor apartment.

The door to the salon was open. She could hear nothing from inside. A small lamp burned on a shelf on the far wall but gave only meager light. As far as she could tell, the room was empty.

Without the light from the crystal chandeliers playing on them, the yellow silk coverings on the hexagonal walls looked shabby. The texture of the rough stone could be seen through the thin fabric. The modern couches and upholstered chairs seemed as anachronistic in the five-hundred-year-old room as the art deco fresco on the ceiling of Geoffredo's apartment. It was as though, in half light, the room reverted to its origin; built to withstand the blows of nature and to outlast its succession of inhabitants.

Floor-to-ceiling windows were in three of the five walls. Two of the windows opened out to the walkway with the balustrade in front of the fresco. One was slightly open and a light wind billowed a white curtain, moving it slowly across the floor and back again like an uncertain dancer.

From where she stood in the doorway, Andrea could not see the makeshift bar where she was afraid she had left the box of *tarocchi*. Weaving her way past twin couches and through a small grouping of straight chairs she reached the table that had earlier held wine and mineral water and plates of food. It had been cleared. The glasses, serving dishes, and bottles were gone. All that remained was a vase with cut flowers that had already begun to wilt. Brownish circles where wet glasses had stood soiled the top of the linen cloth.

The *tarocchi* were not there. The box was either in the safe or Geoffredo had put it somewhere else for safekeeping. Or—Andrea could not ignore the possibility—someone else had found and taken the priceless miniatures.

As she turned to leave she glanced into the mirror behind the bar and saw a reflected bright flash. Could it be that the burning crate was not so harmless after all? Had someone lit it first then touched off a drape or the fabric on the walls of the salon?

Turning quickly, she could see nothing that looked like a fire, but she felt an unexplained wariness.

Again! There it was again. A flash of brilliant orange close to the door. Now it leaped and filled the doorway. It shifted, wavered, then was still.

It was the color of flame. Bright enough, Andrea realized, to be seen at a distance and give warning. It signaled danger—stay away—to anyone who saw it. And it gave protection to the one who wore it. The coverall had drawstrings at the neck, the wrists, and ankles. The hands were covered with gloves of the same orange rubberized material, and a billed cap with a plexiglass shield covered the face and head. The shoes, too, were covered with fabric boots like those worn by a surgeon. But unlike a doctor's protective clothing this uniform was to guard against something more tangible than germs. It was designed to protect the wearer against the deadly insecticide carried in a pouch attached to the front of the belt.

It could have been either a man or a woman. The body was slender, but the height was difficult to judge as measured against the frame of the enormous salon door.

"What the hell are you doing here?" The words were low and muffled.

Andrea stood as still as the figure in the doorway.

"The fire in the vestibule wasn't meant to attract anyone but Geoffredo." What was it in the voice—resignation, regret? The hint of some trampled emotion was trapped inside the plexiglass shield. "The salon seemed a more appropriate setting than his apartment."

One gloved hand automatically reached up to touch the concealed hair, forgetting that it was covered by the cap.

Andrea recognized the gesture. She had seen those fingers comb through the now hidden hair that was as wild and unruly as a lion's mane.

"Carlo?"

He unhooked the visor and looked at her sadly with his Halloween cat's eyes. "Why are you prowling around in the middle of the night?"

It was not just the color of the coveralls that signaled danger. Carlo was guarding the single exit like a goalie in a soccer game. "The *tarocchi*. I wasn't sure what had happened to the box."

"You really didn't know Geoffredo well, did you? If you had, you would have been sure that the miniatures were safely locked away. My brother always lived up to his position as Count Gonzaga; he maintained the past. He would never have let any harm come to a family heirloom."

Carlo was alert, unmoving. But casually, he asked, "Were you going to marry him?"

"No."

"If I could have believed that, this masquerade costume might not have occurred to me."

"Why?"

"My older brother with a new wife, a new family—I couldn't allow that."

She did not answer. Something had happened to Geoffredo. Andrea was as sure of it as she was of her own dangerous situation.

"I told you before I was born out of sequence. That has always been my problem."

Maybe she could keep him talking. Carlo liked to talk. "Do you really believe you've lived before?"

"Ah, the transmigration of souls." Carlo laughed. "Don't you have the feeling that there are past Gonzagas in the room here with us?"

Andrea did not answer.

"No. Truthfully, I never could quite believe," Carlo said. "I wanted to. It's an amusing idea. Speculating on who you might have been in another life is interesting, don't you think? Weren't you rather taken with the idea of having been Lucrezia?"

"No." Minimum answers were all Andrea could manage. She had to think of a way to escape.

"And after I went to all the trouble to find your picture in a back copy of *Art News* so I could put your face on the Duchess of Este's body." A deep sigh lifted his shoulders. Then, almost pathetically, he said, "But it is a good miniature, isn't it."

"Yes. You're a talented artist. I like the one in here, too."

"That was really Sammy's idea ... sending *Afterimage* to Geoffredo, I mean. Sammy had some grandiose idea of stimulating my career—and his commissions—by putting together an exhibit of past and present Gonzaga works of art. Of course Geoffredo wouldn't agree to it." His head turned toward the painting. "It's not a bad painting. Quite good, really, for what it is. That kind of thing has paid the bills. I've done all right. Money is not a problem, never has been. I don't want you to think that's why any of this happened."

Andrea did not ask him to explain. She knew. He had poisoned Geoffredo. Somewhere—maybe in this room— Geoffredo was dead.

"Both Geoffredo and I were fed stories of past glory with our mother's milk. The honor of the Gonzagas, the feud with the Estes. Our father was one of a long line of counts. We grew up in a *castle*. Everything we heard— everything we saw—was a reminder of the propagation of the line, the indestructibility of the name."

Andrea tried to judge the distance between her and the partly open window that led to the outside walkway. Could she get there before Carlo could get to her?

"The irony of it all was that I was more caught up in the historical nonsense than my older brother, but it didn't really apply to me. Because of"—he wrote the word in the air the way he had spelled out Castello di Gonzaga earlier in his room—"primogeniture! The oldest son inherits! The oldest son is the heir! And I was only the second son."

Automatically his hand started toward his hair again. He stopped the gesture midway. "There was a mistake somewhere—I've always known—we were born out of sequence. Even when we were children I used to tell Geoffredo we were born at the wrong time. I should have been born first!"

Andrea took a step backward, putting a couch between her and Carlo. She was sure he noticed, but he did not move.

"The bone I was thrown as a child was, 'If anything happens to Geoffredo, you're second in line.' I hung onto that for years, then buried it in my mind, knowing it was there to dig up sometime. Then he got married. I felt threatened, but my career had begun to take off, and in New York my family didn't seem as important. But still, I was relieved when his wife couldn't produce a living heir."

194

Andrea took a slow step toward the window.

"I'm sorry about the fire this afternoon," Carlo said casually. "That was just a small attempt to spook you."

She ran her hands along the top of the couch, sliding her feet sideways. Her leg touched something solid on the floor. Dreading to—afraid to know—she glanced down. It was Geoffredo. The side of his face was pressed against the carpet—his arms flung out in front of him like a swimmer. Even in the semidarkness she could see light reflected in one bulging eye.

She leaned against the couch, her arms stiff, bracing herself. The horror she had felt at the deaths of the three unknown people earlier was magnified that many times. This was a man she had known. She had kissed those lips that were drawn back so grotesquely now.

The room seemed to revolve. Carlo's feverish voice still reached her from the doorway.

". . . couldn't let you marry him . . ." he was saying. "Caterina was not a threat. Somehow, I always thought I would outlive Geoffredo, and eventually I would be the oldest son. When you're a child, ten years—even five years—seems a huge age difference. But when I saw him this time, I realized it was nothing at all. I could easily die before he did. And he was planning to get married again. And you, my dear, were something out of the ordinary. Any man that married you would want to spend all his time trying to have children. I could imagine a half dozen little Geoffredo Juniors in line for the title of Count Gonzaga before I got a shot at it."

She could never get past Carlo through the door. The window was the only way.

". . . and so I took fate into my own hands—as so many past Gonzagas have done—and saw to the succession myself."

He held out the arms of the orange rubberized suit. "Not exactly dressed in regal robes," he said. "But you see before you a man who is now the oldest son. The heir to the Castello di Gonzaga. Count Carlo Gonzaga the first."

Andrea ran to the window. Carlo did not hurry. He snapped down the visor before he followed her out. It was too far to jump over the balustrade to the ground from this end. The hill sloped away and there was a sharp drop to the vineyard below. She knew how the walkway was constructed. She had planned to work from this very location on the fresco. A box of her equipment stood against the wall. Beside it was a length of aluminum tubing, an extension for a long-handled brush. She grabbed it as the only weapon available.

He was on the walkway now. At least he was easier to see than she was. She crouched down against the castle. Somehow she had to get past him. There was no escape from the walkway. It was closed on both ends, designed only as a decoration on the facade, not as a passageway.

When he found her, all he would have to do was hold the powdered insecticide against her skin a few minutes the way he must have done to Geoffredo. He could grab her wrist, her ankle, her neck!

Carlo walked slowly, feeling his way with one hand against the wall. The other hand was in the pouch at his waist. He obviously could not see well through the tinted visor and tipped it up. But he was in no hurry. He knew he had her trapped.

Andrea wedged the aluminum rod between two stones on the castle wall and braced it on the low ledge of the balustrade. If he tripped and got off balance for a moment, she could crawl past him, then run back through the window and the open door of the salon.

He struck the rod with his shin and stumbled. Instead of

falling against the balustrade as Andrea had expected he would, he dropped to one knee and braced himself against the wall. He was merely thrown off balance for a moment.

Daylight was only minutes away. But lethargic clouds, empty of their snow, stretched thin, gray, and motionless across the sky, darkening the predawn pallor.

Andrea huddled in a deep shadow where the wall jutted forward to meet the corner of the walkway. She knew Carlo could still not see her, nor did he know how little distance there was between them!

Stumbling on the rod had surprised him. He seemed slightly disoriented as he struggled to his feet. The coveralls were clumsy and stiff, and had twisted when he fell. He stood a moment, regaining his bearing. Then, out of the habit of a lifetime, he reached a hand to his uncovered face and tangled black hair.

The moment the powdered poison touched his skin he gasped, then screamed as he tried to run. He tripped a second time on the metal handle that blocked his path.

Men who work with the deadly insecticide know, though Carlo did not, that there is a matter of a few precious minutes after contact when water will wash away certain death. But it was not the TEPP that killed Carlo Gonzaga. In his panic, he lurched forward. Losing his footing, he tumbled over the balustrade.

His head struck the side of the castle as he fell and he was dead before his body landed at the top of the steep slope and rolled down into the wild vines.

Twenty-two

"Are you sure you want to do this?" Aldo Balzani parked his Fiat on a narrow side street across from the University of Ferrara. He waited for Andrea to answer before he got out to open the door.

"Yes," she said.

"If you're sure. It's not far to walk from here."

No one would ever have guessed that there had been ice on the sidewalk the day before. The ground was still wet and the air was chilly, but there was no sign of snow anywhere. The streets looked bright with a still-damp shininess. It was as though the sun had withheld the warmth from yesterday to dispense today. And the birds, chirping excitedly, seemed willing to give spring another try.

Balzani took Andrea's hand and put it with his in the pocket of his wool jacket.

She asked, "Have you talked to the men at the lab?"

"Yes. It looks like our friend the captain was right. There were no signs of tampering with the cork or the seal. The poison must have been in the wine when it was bottled years ago."

They turned the corner past the campus. In front of them was a winding alley, too narrow for cars. On either side were ugly post–World War II houses made of concrete blocks. There was nothing in sight left as a reminder of the former grandeur of Ferrara.

"Did the captain mention the garnet ring?"

"No. Except to say that you told him Caterina has it."

"I mean, did he tell you who took it out of my purse?"

"No."

"Then I may know something he doesn't."

"Oh?"

"Lucio came to talk with me this morning before I left. He's the one who put it on the temporary girl's finger."

"Why?"

"His conscience, I suppose. He had taken the girl to his apartment the night before, and he wasn't very proud of the way he had treated her. He said he had made fun of her when she claimed to be an Este."

"Not that again."

"Talk to your friend, the captain. He'll explain why that is still so important to some local people."

"But why the ring?"

"He was the first one to find the girl's body, but he was afraid to tell anyone. All he could think of was that he may have been the last person to see her alive. He was afraid he'd jeopardize his job—or maybe even be accused of her death if he got involved by reporting it. But then, the more he thought about it, the worse he felt. He had seen me with the ring that afternoon at the studio. And after several glasses of wine at the reception, he took it out of my purse on an impulse and put it on the girl's finger. He said she was very proud of her hands. She kept her nails perfectly, and always polished. And while he was just a little drunk, he thought how happy it would have made her to wear the ring of an Este countess—at least for a little while."

The building they were looking for was not marked. It was hidden behind a high wall. A young woman in a tattered machine-made sweater was sweeping the sidewalk in front of her house. They stopped and asked her for directions.

"The Convent of Corpus Domini? Yes. Yes, that is it." She pointed. "But you will have to knock on the gate several times. The sisters are all old and it takes them a long time to answer."

Andrea and Balzani thanked her and did as she suggested. As they waited, Balzani asked, "What happens to the Gonzaga castle and winery now that both Geoffredo and Carlo are dead?"

"Tess, Carlo's stepdaughter, is the heir."

"It will be interesting to see what happens."

"Lucio, I'm sure, will be delighted to help her. And Murray Eastman, her grandfather, will probably stay on. If anyone knows about wine distribution, he does. Strange," Andrea said and locked her fingers inside Balzani's, "the castle no longer belongs to either a Gonzaga or an Este."

"It's just as well."

After a few minutes, two figures stood at the gate. Their faces were hidden by hoods that were pulled down to their mouths.

Andrea explained why they had come, and the two nuns led them through a neglected courtyard, into the convent by the back way, and into the church.

It was dark and cold and smelled musty as though the air in the small sanctuary had been trapped there for centuries. One of the black-clad figures pointed in the direction of the nun's choir, then stood quietly by the door, waiting.

In front of the altar were several tombs of ordinary gray stone. On one was the name "Alfonso I." Next to it was a smaller one and the lettering was less distinct. Andrea could read what was written there, but she knelt down and spelled out the letters with her fingers, "Lucrezia Borgia, Duchess of Este."

She was not sure why she had wanted to come here. But a sense of peace and kinship seemed to flow through her body from the stone she touched.

Andrea and Aldo Balzani stayed only a few minutes. When they left, they gave the nuns money for the alms box.

Outside the air was fresh and clean and the sun had never seemed brighter. "I'm starved," Andrea said.

"The captain says Nandina's is the best place in town for capelletti."

When they were seated at a sidewalk table with a checkered cloth and a bottle of local red wine in front of them, Andrea was still thinking of the Duchess of Este. She hoped there had been a few days like this for Lucrezia. Days when the sun warmed her face and arms and a cool wind ruffled her hair as she looked across the rim of her glass at a man she loved.